NIGHT DRIVING

NIGHT DRIVING

STORIES BY JOHN VANDEZANDE

To Tom Dibble —
All my best
John VandeZande
7-26-90

ARBOR HOUSE
WILLIAM MORROW
New York

Library of Congress Cataloging-in-Publication Data

VandeZande, John.
Night driving: stories / by John VandeZande.
p. cm.
ISBN 1-55710-051-9
I. Title.
PS3572.A4293N5 1989
813'.54—dc20

89-6907
CIP

Printed in the United States of America

First Edition

1 2 3 4 5 6 7 8 9

BOOK DESIGN BY MARK STEIN

For Elaine

ACKNOWLEDGMENTS

Some of the stories in this book originally appeared in the following periodicals and anthologies: *The Ghent Quarterly* and *Small Winter Wars,* "The Sound of the Lafayette Escadrille"; *Fiction Network Magazine,* "Night Driving"; "Coming Ashore"; "Swimming"; "Child Rearing"; *The Michigan Quarterly Review* and *The Third Coast: Contemporary Michigan Fiction,* "Fox Feed."

CONTENTS

To be able to experience and live out capacities for tender love requires the confronting of the daimonic.

—Rollo May
Love and Will

NIGHT DRIVING

Chores done, Lonnie Pershing pulls his flame-striped Chevy out of his father's driveway and onto the flat, dark Wisconsin highway. Behind him the farm's breathing barns and still machinery lie waiting for him, for tomorrow, for the rest of his life, but tonight, after a day steeped in sun and grain-dusted sweat, a day against the angular sun arming down, tonight is . . . tonight. Two hundred animals fold down into sleep behind him as he hits it, hits the Chevy into first and spits the last of his father's gravel out of his tires' cleats back into his driveway, against the high silos and machine sheds, the tethered bull and the pliant cows, *nails it,* and hears, feels, first gear's roar out of the headers and the glass-packed mufflers. The road is dark. Redlining, he comes out of low at 5500 on the tach and catches second's sweet song and channels it along with the song on WKLS and finds high at eighty, high's sweet register in another key, and *goes.*

She is out there somewhere in the living fields, the fields around him in their mile-long rows, their deep manures and turned earth, black elms against a heat-lit sky; she is out there somewhere, and against this fact, he drives.

His headlights cut into the night's dark and into this white wound he drives. The engine throbs through the floor and up his legs while the wind's whine at the window brings the heavy night into him.

Outside, the fields of corn and grain are deep into themselves. Heat lightning flares down a far field and thunder says that somewhere there may be rain. In the woodlots and the living fences of Lombardy and oak and elm, owls and nighthawks sit high and unblinking, seeing with night eyes their ground-bound prey and taking their time.

Lonnie drives. His hands lie lightly on the wheel, kid-glove handling like she will need. Seven miles to go and he is torn between the twin pleasures of her and driving. He knows both, but driving is sure where she is not. Driving is not moody, does not sulk down into the knotted complications of family and times of month and morals and a dark German church with its flesh-hating laws and long arm of influence.

He drives. WKLS plays his favorite song, then fades, fainter, fades, is gone (a socket of silence, longer than a day in the fields), then returns, clears, swells, and is back again. Holly carbs spurt gas through their jets.

His sun- and razor-rawed face stings beneath the after-shave, and he leans into the open window to cool it. He would rather have come to her straight from the fields and the vibrating tractor, but he knows her. She wants quiet words and soft moves, good smells, and time. She wants, always wants, a tangle of complications: to know his past and have him know hers, her wishes, her fears, her private thoughts and even more private dreams; all this she wants in the cramp of the front seat where he has parked on a line where someone's field meets a woodlot, where the Chevy's hood is buried in the wood's darkness and moon slides down its trunk. In the daytime, when he is in the fields or up in a loft in a sun-slatted barn or hooking cows to the milking machines, he dreams of means to get around, get past, the talk and to the point. To him, all of that is so much backing and filling, but she wants it and so the after-shave and some rehearsed words, some stored-away strategic questions ("What do you dream about?" "When you go to church, do you talk to God?" "If you could do whatever you wanted, what do you think you would do?"), and some techniques with words like *manipulation* and *zones* from "What Women Want" in this month's *Male,* now buried deep between mattress and springs, back beyond where the blankets fold under, beyond his mother's farthest reach in her Monday morning cleaning. A magazine whose pages speak to him with the power to conjure. Drives.

And passes her church. Against the dark sky and darker fields it stands sternly up. Crossed at the top, it is narrow and severe like the minister himself. At its side is a small cemetery, its gray, cold stones jutting squarely out of the ground dotting the tree-scattered hill with death, a reminder that if the words she hears there each Sunday about flesh and sin and their wages are not enough, she need only look out the window to see the proof of what the minister says. He has waited for her there on hot Sunday noons and seen her white look as she crossed the parking lot with lowered eyes to his car. Her father stands looking toward the car, his arms crossed. The sight of her and those sun-bitten, bound-down-in-Sunday-clothes farmers on the porch shaking hands with a man who has not done a day's work in his life, a man they have to their houses for dinner, a man they pay to make them feel bad besides, baffles him. At 105 he throttles down for the half-mile to her house. The glass packs sound off across the fields as he gears down. At her father's driveway, he goes down to first gear and lays off the gas. He wants her to hear him but not her father.

In her driveway, the Chevy idling heavily, nosed up between the house and machine shed, he waits. The sky is low. He hears the thunder louder now. Fifteen miles away at the crossroad the guys are probably washing their cars in the rain at Kedd's Full-Service and cooling their beer in the back room. Their cars are soaped and rain-slicked under the neon lights and the oil on the cement drive is making rainbows in the water. Talking shit. Killing time. Playing grabass and snapping washrags and wet leather chamois. On the highway out front the over-the-road truckers they know are laying on the horns as they roll by.

In the spill of his headlights her father's house is a tall, dull white against the night. It could be a lighthouse and the fields an ocean. Tall windows let out long squares of light into the yard. A frog squawks in a drain ditch. He waits for her to come out of the house. If she has seen or heard him and if her father is sleeping in his chair in front of the TV, she will be out in minutes. He would blow the horn or go to the door, but this could rekindle whatever it is deep within her father that the minister speaks to, whatever fiery place is fueled by a displeasure with life that not even dawn-to-dusk farm work can quench. He has seen him redden her face with a slap that sent her into a barn wall, and he has seen him slit a piglet's throat and hang it on a fence and press a tin cup to the jumping wound as if he were drawing water from a tap. The rocks he plows up from his fields are no harder.

Staring over the wheel, he wills her out. Simple waiting has changed into a fierce willing, a concentrated effort that allows him to see through the house, its siding, studs, the walls themselves, and into that room where she lives and he has never entered. There, in the center of soft things and softer colors, amid smells foreign to a farm, she moves with a grace and familiarity he thinks he will never know. He silently commands her to leave the house, to give her father a wide berth where he sleeps in the chair, to avoid her mother's eyes and appear in the light from the kitchen door. Toward the end of his vigil, when he all but fears that the effort of his willing will spend him, she appears. In a light, full sleeveless dress she eases the screen door back into its frame and, that fast, is across the yard and into his car. He checks the impulse to race the motor and backs out onto the highway.

She is golden in the lights from the dashboard. Her fullness strains her clothes. Her perfumed woman-smell fills the car and settles like dew on the seats, his face, his hand on the wheel. She is settled in the hollow of his arm, and his left hand guides the wheel by fingertip, his right hand on the globy roundness of her upper arm. Her hair smells of soap and flowers and its touch soothes his face. The click of the road-seams keeps the music's time.

Barely idling alongside a living fence of scrub and brush dividing fields, the Chevy crests small waves of fallow furrows, geared down, rumbling its way along the field's edge, looking. A woodlot of aspen opens, and they enter. The Chevy's lights black out and the trees and the night drape down. From above, the sky lets pale light down through the dark leaves and dapples their faces and hands. Her face is in shards as it comes up to his, a puzzle to be put together by feel. In the dark he moves out on this expanse of white and, his eyes closed, his mouth explores her face like an expedition on a new continent. Finding the heat of her mouth, he settles there and he knows what death is. It is a dissolving, a giving-over; it is like the stories he has heard of men caught out in Wisconsin winter storms found frozen to death in peaceful sleep, propped against fence posts and trees, their faces showing no sign of struggle, rather, at rest, reposed, as if the cold were something to lie down into. Buttons hold like burrs. His callused hands catch on silk and tiny clasps slip the pliers of his fingers. His journey through layers of cloth seems to take ages, in terror, in forlornness, in love, and in awe.

Abject, he could believe in God. He talks now, but too late and with so little breath. ("What do you dream about?" "Do you ever see God's face?" "Could you go away like Catholics to live with women?") In the sibilance of her dressing while hunched over the seat, her silence in response to his questions is heavy. Though he cannot name it *remorse,* he can sense it as it forms itself like gathering cloud-shapes that fill the Chevy's small space. He has felt it before here in the car on other nights, and one day earlier this summer in the fields. He had been plowing a half-mile from the house and outbuildings when the sky had begun to darken and lower. No wind had seemed to drive the clouds; rather they had appeared from no source or direction. Over him they had roiled and thickened and pushed him down. While around him the fields had lost their light in minutes and had gone from the color of salmon to barnwood, he had sat on the tractor stalled between rows. He had felt it then—a pressure he knew to be a storm warning but a meaning that struggled to rise up in him in words, but for which he had none of his own. What words there were were someone else's, her father's, maybe, or the minister's, and they would not form in his mind. What he had felt then in the fields and felt now in the car was a vastness, a sensation of too much space, even though it crowded him. Too much space and, no matter how far he might reach in all directions, no one he could touch.

She has not answered his questions, and her bright silence tells him that she knows them for what they are. Dressed now, she is again shrouded in mystery. The dim sounds she makes from the far corner of the seat are wounded, and in the dark he thinks of the small pipings of rabbits and gophers turning under the tractor's wheels or behind him somewhere in the machinery's steel.

Her voice has in it small, heavy things that weight it and bring it down. He can do nothing to lift it. His face smoldering from their recent heat, he is at a loss.

Back on the road, the driving eases him and the Chevy calms him in its perfect running. Like all machinery, it can be fixed and has this advantage. Its weight and resistance, its iron solidity, can be legislated against by pushing or pulling harder. Pulling the Chevy's engine and slinging it in the barn rafters with something as simple as a hand-cranked come-along, seeing it hanging and turning in its down-seeking mass from a bowed rafter, creates in him a feeling too real to ever be outside itself and see itself as joy. Should he be given to see one thing as another, he would know the pleasure a straight plowed row brings to his father. Parked in her driveway, he watches her walk toward her father's house.

It's a straight shot to Kedd's Korners. One time through the gears at just under redline and he's there, the fifteen miles vanishing behind him as if they hadn't been. Distance has never been a problem for the Chevy, merely a matter of space to be eclipsed at whatever speed the traffic will bear. Tonight the road is all but empty, a gift. He gears down for his approach.

Kedd's is dark. He has missed closing time by no more than five minutes, five minutes that would have told him *where to now, what happens next.* There are a half-dozen places where the guys could be, but they are in all directions from Kedd's, somewhere out and among the squared fields. He crawls in first gear in and around the islands of pumps under the unlit neon banks, nosing the Chevy here and there, looking for a sign. None. Only the sting of gas in the air and its slick on the puddles show there has just been someone here. To the side of the station on the oil-soaked gravel, Pedersen's GTO sits with its hood up, its blown 405 hanging over the engine hole from a pine pole tripod. Inside the garage, up on a hoist, a pickup is perched in the air, its exhaust system hanging down like spilled guts. Around the other side of the station, by the tourist bathrooms, are some empty barrels that have been there for as long as he can remember. Everyone is gone. He turns the Chevy and heads it out to the highway. If nothing else, he thinks, he will leave a mark. Clutch in, he holds the gas pedal to the floor and leans out his open door to watch the back wheels. When he pops the clutch, the Chevy hangs for a moment in a screaming, smoking stasis and then fishtails up the highway, leaving behind twin esses of black on the pavement. A small thing, it satisfies. Manning's Ford would have blown a tranny laying rubber like that.

The rain is gone now. His father in the morning will say, "Not enough, just enough on top for the sun's heat to burn. Better off without it." His father will roust him at four, bitter, filling his bedroom door in his same clothes, and tell him, as if he hadn't heard it before and didn't know, that there is work to be done before breakfast. His father who walks out on the land each morning as if it is a penance, who puts on a mask of grief along with his pants and shirt. He is not like her father; rather, he is a man who acts as if he wishes he were never born. Lonnie has not seen his father touch his mother.

Overhead the sky is high again, the clouds gone. The highway ahead accomplishes by yards as he and the Chevy look for whatever there is to look for. There is Bergdahl to the east on 557—a water tower sticking up out of a thin scattering of lights; to the west, nothing for miles within this night's driving; south is Kedd's, and north is home. Though the driving soothes, it brings with it now thoughts of what kind of man he will be, like his father or hers, and if there is something that makes of everything a sadness or guilt or rage. He had not meant tonight to be like it was. His moves had offended. They, like his thoughts and his body's feelings, were too fast and not under his control. They had had the speed of her father's hand across her face, the speed and force of a storm over fields that, before you knew it, caught you up in the center of itself.

He had meant the night to be slower and smoother with the talk she wanted, but his past and his wishes and dreams, what she wanted to talk about, have been merely a waiting for *tomorrow.* There had been no face in his fantasies. She had brought one, and tonight as she turned toward him she again put a face on his dreams, and in this way she made tomorrow *today* and he rushed out to meet it. Though he always thinks he will, he does not think of the pictures in the magazine when he is with her. Now he cannot remember what they look like—the faces and bodies that when the rest of the house is asleep burn themselves into his eyes.

On the edge of Bergdahl the yellow blinking light hanging over the road slows him, and once past it he floors the Chevy. The speedometer winds up to the right and down through the high numbers. He passes farms now with small gnarled orchards up close to the houses, kids' corn-selling stands next to the road, mailboxes with reflectors on their posts to mark driveways. At the edge of a field two whitetail does look up from the grasses where they nose in their girlish ease and then, unafraid but shy, put their heads down again. He would tell her of his memories and dreams—of the popping sound a cat made when it had lain down by a sleeping cow for warmth in the winter and the cow had rolled over on it; of the Mexican migrant worker's son who had awakened to find his father with his throat slit, the bed full of blood, the razor still in his hand; of the sounds his mother had made in her room when she had his youngest sister too fast to be taken to the hospital. He would tell her but he cannot, they are too frightening, too black to be talked about, too much part of the inside of him. He imagines a place where they could be and she holds him and rocks him, but what would he say to her? That he dreams of soft fields where they make love, then lie back to trace the shapes of clouds? These dreams come to him now, but he puts them out of his mind as childish and foolish. The men he knows would not tell of such things.

On the straightaway up ahead some clown comes at him with his high beams on. Lonnie flicks his own high beams on and off to let him know, but the other lights don't change; they bear steadily on. Lonnie flicks his a few more times and then with a gratifying flick leaves them on high. As he strains to look to the right of the searing glare, they continue coming on toward him and then they pass each other in a moment of white blackout, horns blaring, and then each is past the other, their moment of blind faith over. In his rearview mirror the taillights disappear. It is time to head home.

At the four-way stop he and the Chevy idle down, Lonnie breathless. The fields around are flatter, darker, and the heavy night air with its smells of fertile furrows and damp grasses comes into the car to him. *Left* is home. Right is three days' driving to Florida, or the Grand Canyon or Los Angeles with its cherry cars. Right is oceans or anything in your mind. Right is where the music on the radio comes from, *places* that can be reached on three tanks of gas.

He turns left. Two miles down the road and there is her house again. He pulls into her driveway and kills the lights. Her window is a dim square in the upper story. He waits without hope, fearing a light in a lower window. Then, she is there—one hand lifted to the side of her face, where it moves, a benediction, and then she is gone and the light goes out.

For a moment he sits in awe of where she had appeared and then he swings the Chevy out onto the road.

WKLS plays an old song, two months old on the charts, and Lonnie heads for home. Its familiar words and rhythm ease him, the Chevy fills with the size of the music, and for a mile down the road he is at rest. The words are comfortable and he knows them: *you* and *blue, tonight, all right.* They come to mind easily and he sings along with the radio. Too soon, the song is over. The DJ would sell him some acne medicine and Lonnie punches a button to another station. It's playing a fast one, another of his favorites, and he turns it up and floors the Chevy. Tomorrow he'll get up before his father, and he will try to talk to her, just talk, about anything she wants. He backs the Chevy off for a curve, powers through it, and then, bringing it to an even hundred, he holds it there all the way home.

Coming Ashore

Dawn on Lake Superior was a tarnished-silver lifting of sea and sky around their small boat where the three of them sat cramped between tackle boxes and life rings and nets, their knees at times touching as they turned, their shoulders hunched. On the horizon, where the sun was making up to become a ball, the silver shone dully and then, above it and the lake's low haze, polished out to a lighter blue. Against these faded washes an early roaming flock of sea gulls accompanied them out with a high, rhythmic white winking.

In the bow, Kellan's ten-year-old son trailed his fingertips over the side, raising a tiny wake of his own, which bubbled in the light swells. The boy was still sleepy and that, coupled with his awkwardness in the life preserver, made Kellan a little nervous. He would have said something, but he did not want to spoil the boy's play. Finally, when the boy reached for an object floating a few feet out from the bow and made the boat lurch slightly, Kellan had to tell him. "Paulie," he said, looking past his father where he sat on the middle seat. "Keep your hands in the boat."

Paulie turned on the seat and centered himself. In his man-size orange life preserver he bulked forward and leaned into an embarrassed agreement, which said, *yes, they were about a man's business here, he had forgotten, and he was sorry.* The embarrassment brought his elbows down to rest on his knees and his eyes to stare at the boat's floor. To ease him, Kellan caught Paulie's eye and smiled. Paulie smiled back and it was all right again.

"Alaska," Kellan's father said, not looking back at

the boy, "you do that, put your hands in that water, and they cut open a dog's gut and stick your hands in so they don't freeze and fall off. And they *would* freeze. Just like chunks of ice. Superior ain't any different from that Alaska water."

With this new knowledge the boy took up and held his wet hand in his dry one and gazed out over the lake as if he were looking into pages far ahead in his arithmetic book. His face pulled into a tight frown as he struggled to equate water and ice and this new, furthest integer, a dog's stomach. Failing to find the answer, he put an unbelieving question to his grandfather's back. "In his stomach, Grampa?"

"That's right. In his cut-open gut. To get at that blood. It's the only thing that'll match your own blood's temperature and keep it from freezing. You ask your dad if that ain't right."

"Like Tippy?" Paulie was staring straight over his grandfather's back at Kellan, and Kellan could see that it had gone too far. The boy was beyond puzzlement now and into the terror of a strange truth brought home, made too familiar. He was too young, and prone to bad dreams. "No, not like Tippy, Paulie," he said. "Not like Tippy. They're *special* dogs. They have like zippers in them. They're real special dogs."

"Special?" The boy's face, even though he didn't completely understand, relaxed now. *Special* carried it out and beyond the fenced-in familiar, carried it into the fantastic—TV shows, videos, bionic toys. The set look on Grampa's face said that he didn't agree with this deception, but Kellan had to go against him on this one. Paulie was too young just yet. Kellan looked out over the lake.

A morning fog, which earlier looked as if it might block the trip, was completely gone now. Behind them, diminishing out away from their wake, the harbor lay still in the calm waters on the other side of the breakwater. Beyond it the town grew small and its houses ranked up its hills in fading colors, smaller still. Those on the hills nearest the shoreline were old, turn-of-the-century houses, three-storied, heavily scrolled, some with widow's walks, fretwork. If this were eighty years ago, Kellan knew, women would be there on watch. But it wasn't, and this was Saturday, and he knew that the town was still asleep.

The motor's roar rose and fell as the lake lifted and lowered the stern up and over the rounding swells. Small pieces of late-spring ice rose at the edges as they topped the foot-high swells and rocked toward shore. Grampa, wedged into his task, fingered some springing line from a tackle box between his feet. He was a big man, recently retired, and plying coil from coil of near-invisible monofilament fishing line, he looked as if his strength had somehow traveled to his fingertips and there had been changed to patience. Never jerking or pulling at the doubling coils, he separated one from another and served the straightened line onto a spool propped against his boot.

Ahead of them, a mile up the coastline, lay their destination, the mouth of the best rainbow-trout river in the county. At this time of the year the fish were lying off the mouth in the lake, waiting for the temperature to rise and signal the start of their spring spawning run upriver. From this distance the mouth was a darker gap in the shoreline of rock and evergreens. Out from it the heavy snow and soil runoff stained the water a light brown for a quarter-mile until it gradually paled and ran clean, in ripples. Kellan gave the throttle a quarter-turn.

Twenty minutes of hard running put them out beyond the runoff waters. There were no other boats on the lake. This could mean that the temperature was not right and that there were no fish. Or it could mean that they had the jump on any other fishermen and would be free to move from one spot to another without fear of fouling someone else's lines. That would make for a perfect morning. Kellan believed it. So did his father, who showed it with a small roll of his shoulder and a look in his eyes. A little over a quarter mile out, Kellan throttled down and they anchored.

From this far out the shore was a dark line against the blue. Back down the line the town was a crosshatched mat of squares, rectangles, and triangles against the snow-streaked hills rounding up behind it. Closer to the boat, mallards mixed in with gulls bobbing in the swells. Green and russet and ringed around the neck, the mallards' colors, land colors, were bold against the water's blue and the gulls' white, which repeated on the waves' crests lipping in toward shore.

They began by bottom-fishing. The boat rolled lightly on the small swells, ranging and stretching on the anchor line as they hunched deeper into their clothes against the stilled chill of sitting. They had agreed that if the trout weren't in close, they would head out a little and troll.

In a half-hour nothing had happened, and as his father brought up the anchor, Kellan turned in his seat to adjust the outboard.

The lake was making up a bit out of the northwest when they headed out. Another five hundred feet and they were into trolling waters. The sea birds hadn't followed them. The birds stayed close to shore, where they could pick up surface cripples in the shallower waters. Grampa rigged the lines, one steel deep line over the stern and surface rods over the sides.

Kellan put them into a downshore troll and eased into a slow run parallel to the shoreline. Grampa had turned to face the bow and was fishing over the side, playing his surface line with a few jerks to bring the lure up, then letting it slack off to change the action. From the front seat, Paulie watched over his shoulder and imitated his grandfather's moves with his own rod. Kellan's rod, running the deep line over the stern, was locked into a clamp on the gunwale. He watched the tip for a strike.

Later, when he was in the water and had time to think, when he wasn't trying to throw off the impossible cold or kick to keep the overturned boat pointed toward shore, Kellan would think of it as a mindless conspiracy: Grampa's shouting that he had a *strike,* Paulie's pitching toward Grampa's side to *see,* the renegade wave moving under the bow. Kellan had been quartering the waves, picking up the bow at a forty-five, and then dishing into the oncoming trough to ride the next one up when it happened. He remembered no other sounds than *strike* and *see.* Then the bow had plunged and they were out in the water.

For a few seconds Kellan was pulled down and under the capsized boat, but then by kicking and thrashing, he came up alongside and reached for a hold on the boat's bottom. His fingers found the keel, an inch-high ridge of aluminum he hadn't known was there. He was shaking in the bone-numbing cold of the water and air when his father came up on the other side of the boat and grabbed at the keel next to where Kellan hung on. Over the rounding of the boat's bottom they looked at each other. Neither of them spoke. An empty Thermos bottle floated past Kellan's face and bumped off the bow. A few yards away a life ring made an orange *O* on the water and rocked in its trough. The boat was in a trough between two swells and seemed not to move. Kellan swung away from the boat, hanging on with one hand to look around and behind him. This low in the water, the swells rolled in his face and he had to throw himself up on the side of the boat to see. "Paulie," he shouted. There was no answer. He pulled himself, half-swimming, to the stern. He still couldn't see him. "Paulie. Paulie, where are you?"

Then Kellan heard him. Paulie's voice was almost lost in the water's noise. "I'm over here, Daddy. I'm over here."

"Where? I can't see you."

"Over here."

"Are you all right?"

"I'm all right, but I'm cold. I'm so cold, Daddy."

"Keep your head up, Paulie. Lay on your back and let your life preserver hold you. Where are you?"

"I'm here." Behind Kellan, the boy loomed on the crest of a small swell and was pitched toward him in his large life preserver like a chip on the water. The preserver kept him afloat, but he couldn't swim in it, couldn't control it. Kellan reached for him. Holding on to the boat with one hand, Kellan leaned out and reached for him but missed. He reached again and grabbed hold of the preserver by a trailing strap and pulled him up to the boat's side. "The ridge," Kellan shouted. "Grab hold of the ridge." The boy scrambled in his arms, and Kellan slid down into the water and levered him up the side of the boat. Paulie's fingers found the ridge and Kellan told him to hang on. "Just hang on, Paulie."

Across the hull from Kellan, his father said nothing, but his face grayed against his already dark lips. His eyes were deep in his face and one large vein beat in the cup of his left temple. He had lost his hat when he had gone under and his few strands of hair streaked his face. His thick fingers clawed the keel, and when they slipped and gripped again, Kellan said quietly to just hang on.

From his side Kellan tried to pull and kick the boat around so that it would go with the swells toward shore, but it was awash and he couldn't do it by himself. His boots weighted him down, and he tried to push them off by rubbing one against the other. The left one came off. "Dad," he said, "hang on and kick. Turn her. Paulie?" He could hardly talk.

"I'm trying, Dad."

"That's good, Paulie. That's good. Don't let go. Just don't let go. We're going to be all right."

At times Kellan could hardly see his father as he slipped lower in the water, weighted by his woollen clothes. His father's hands reached far out of his mackinaw where it rode up his arms as he slowly slid down. Then his knuckles would tighten as he struggled to pull himself back up to the tiny ridge. Over the boat's rounded bottom his face would come up, moonlike, and he would strain to throw his chest up on the side and then lie there, choking for breath. With the rocking, he couldn't hang on and would slip down again until only his hands showed, knuckles whitening, his watch crystal filled with water. "Dad, for God's sake, pull," Kellan shouted. "Pull." His father's face rose up again and flattened against the boat's bottom.

With his father half out of the water and no longer such a strong drag on the other side, Kellan kicked on his side of the boat and managed to bring the bow around. No longer crossways in the trough, the boat bellied up the next swell but caught and held there, and then slipped back again into the trough, where it rocked. Kellan told them to hang on. Paulie said he was cold. Kellan said yes, yes, he knew. He knew that he was cold. It was very cold, but just to hang on and stay up out of the water. Grampa said nothing. Then Kellan remembered.

The anchor must have spilled out when they capsized and still be hanging into the water, a dead weight on a twenty-foot rope. "Dad? Paulie?" Kellan shouted to both of them. "I've got to go after the anchor and cut it free. It's holding us. You two just hang on and I'll be right up. Just hang on, you hear?" They nodded. Kellan moved down the boat toward the bow and pushed up on the boat's side until he sank into the sheering cold. He came up under the boat into the air space between the front and middle seats. Things floated there: plastic containers from the tackle boxes, bobbers, coils of line, lures. As he reached to find the anchor rope in the cold gloom and then to dig his knife from his pants' pocket, things brushed his face. Loops of line webbed in his hair. A bass lure wobbling in its gangs of hooks tugged at his ear, then floated free. Something bigger, cellophane, plastered to his cheek and he rubbed it away with his free hand. He sawed at the rope until it fell away and the anchor went down. The bow rose slightly and he sank once more to come up on the outside. He looked across the bottom at his father and Paulie and they nodded. His fingers found the ridge.

Against the shoreline and the snow-streaked hills beyond, sea birds flew downshore. First a scattering of gulls whipped up off the lake, followed by a line of stretch-necked ducks, which arrowed behind them on quick wings until Kellan couldn't see them anymore. He had stopped kicking now and rested with his hands stretched over his head, gripping the ridge. A small skin of ice the size of a card table rocked in a trough a few yards away. It rode up the shoreside swell, crested, caught, rocked there like a thing insane, then slipped over the next swell and was gone. Kellan's cheek was stuck to the aluminum. He could have slept in the cold.

How long he hung in the down-dragging cold he didn't know. Only his hands cramping on the ridge seemed to be alive. The rest of him hung with the sureness and down-seeking mass of a plumb bob into the impossible thing that had happened. His eyes kept wanting to close, and when he finally fought them open and lifted his head to see, the skin on his cheek came away and stayed with the boat. He hadn't felt it leave, and when he saw it stuck to the aluminum, it could have been a license or a decal. His eyes were open now and he was back from wherever he had been. He called to Paulie with a question in his voice.

"I'm okay," Paulie said from up on the bow.

"Dad?" Kellan called.

His father's voice was small. Kellan couldn't understand what he was saying. To his father's hands he said, "Stay with us, Dad." Then he called to his son. "Paulie, you okay?"

"I'm okay, but I'm so cold, Daddy. I'm so cold."

"I know, Paulie, I know," Kellan said. "But just hang on. We're not out far. We'll be all right."

Kellan kicked at times, kicked with his bootless foot and tried to hold the boat's bow so that it pointed shoreward. It was too cold to speak when it wasn't necessary, so they rode the boat in silence, each tucked into whatever warm cove his thoughts could find. The boat rocked.

From somewhere far off Kellan heard Paulie's voice. "Daddy." The voice was faint. "Daddy, Grampa's slipping down again. Daddy."

Kellan was back. His fingers slowly uncramped from the ridge and he started to move down the boat's side. As he made his way around the stern, gas and oil from the upturned motor ran over his face and into his mouth. His father's shoulders were barely out of the water, and as the boat rocked in the trough, his chin went under. Kellan pushed away from the boat and came around behind him. "When I lift, grab higher up. Get your chest up on the boat if you can." Kellan took a deep breath and let himself sink the length of his father's body. He closed his eyes against the cold and dug his hands into his father's hips. With nothing to push against but the water, he thrashed with his legs while struggling to grip the wet, hard wool and push his father up. His father's feet thrashed against Kellan's legs and his weight bore them both down. Kellan let himself sink and grabbed his father's sagging body lower down. He had him around the legs now and, with his face pressed to the backs of his father's calves, he threw his shoulders and back against the dead weight and pushed and willed him up the side of the boat. Above Kellan's head the blue was becoming lighter and then he was out, and he took a long shattering breath that he had needed but had forgotten in the numbing cold. He pushed again as his father pulled and crawled his way up the side of the boat and then the boat had him. Kellan hung on until he could breathe evenly again. His father lay on the boat struggling for air. Kellan let go then and went hand over hand around the stern and pulled himself up on the other side to balance his father's weight.

The boat rolled slowly over a swell and dipped into the next trough. Kellan kicked, a mindless, easy sideways push. The boat began to breast the next swell. For a time it surged and rocked forward, then it caught and rocked back. Kellan kicked again, but when the boat slipped back, he did not kick anymore. Overhead, the sky was a long, blue rounding that held everything that Kellan could see. From a power plant downshore a line of smoke went up and then disappeared inland.

A sea gull settled in the water near Kellan, then paddled toward something a few yards away. The gull stabbed with its beak and in two pulsing jerks of its lifted throat swallowed it down. From its walleye it watched Kellan and then thrashed its way into the air again. Its flight was a low, unerring white beating toward shore. Kellan felt sleepy. He feared the sleep because he knew what it might mean, that the cold was taking him.

Across from him, his father stared with dull, near-sightless eyes. Out of the endless blue around them, their blue caught Kellan and drew him into what they knew, and then he knew it too. Against it, denying it, he kicked and then kicked again. As his father's face slipped down and out of sight, Kellan called to him, "Dad, hang on. Jesus, just hang on."

"Daddy, Grampa's slipping down again."

"I know, Paulie," Kellan said. "I know. You just hang on. It'll be all right. You hang on tight."

"I will, Daddy, but I'm so cold it's hard to hang on."

"I know, Paulie, but you just hang on."

Kellan watched his father's fingers, their dark tips whitened with strain, as they slowly uncurled and withdrew from the ridge. The boat surged upward as his father's weight left it.

Over Kellan's head the sky whirled. Blue lightened to white and marbled into darker openings between the lower clouds. Staring up, Kellan hung into the cold.

They didn't all have to die.

The thought held him and, like the swells, rocked him. His father was gone. His son was too young. Soon they would all be gone. *They didn't all have to die.* Paulie was hanging on, but he was weak and cold and couldn't swim in his life preserver. It could maybe take him into shore, but would there be time in the cold? *They didn't all have to die.*

Kellan pushed out and away from the boat. Alone, swimming. Long, strong reachings to grab and haul the water under and past him, reachings to cut the swells and haul them behind, to thrash through the troughs. He was swimming with his strong arms and chest. With his powerful kicks, his other boot came off, and he struggled to throw off his coat. His arms, lighter now, plunged into the swells, which were helping to carry him to shore. Freed from the boat, he could have flown. On the beach, someone waved both arms. A fire blazed high against the trees. They had no boats, but they were ready for him. He was out and away and headed in.

Far behind him, Paulie's voice, thin and small, was calling. Paulie. Paulie on the boat. "Dad? Daddy? Daddy, where are you going?"

Paulie. Kellan turned in the water and saw Paulie

back on the boat. The waves, as he faced into them, tipped him over and he strained to right himself against their rolling power, which was taking him to shore but away from Paulie. He shook his head, trying to clear the cold and the daze. Paulie was out there, high and small and orange, on the boat, which bobbed like a child's toy. The stern rose and Kellan couldn't see him. Then the bow came up and he could see Paulie lying with his body tight to the ridge. The sea was taking him sideways, away from Kellan. The sound of Paulie's voice came over the water, but not his words. Kellan called to him, "I'm coming, Paulie, I'm coming. Hang on."

To get to him, to get beyond the falling walls of water, Kellan would have to climb them or go under them and go back out to sea. He dove and swam with his eyes closed. Five or six times he surfaced for air, until at last when he came up in a trough and looked around, the boat was only a dozen yards away. He dug into the waves and pulled toward it, the boat seeming to recede just beyond his fingertips.

Then he was beside it and reaching up its side to find and hang on to the ridge. Paulie lay there, and Kellan turned his face to his. "Daddy?" Paulie said.

"I was going for help, Paulie," Kellan said. "Just hang on."

"But Daddy."

"What, Paulie? What is it?" Maybe it was better to keep the boy talking.

"Daddy, I'm scared."

"Yeah, I know, Paulie. I am too. It's all right to be scared."

"Yeah, but I think Grampa's under the boat. I think I heard him bumping."

Under the boat again, Kellan saw his father's body washing and surging against the seats and gunwales. Kellan cradled his father's head against further battering as he struggled to bring him to the shortened anchor rope and serve it through his heavy belt. When it was tied off, he pushed himself free and then he was out from under the boat and in the air. He took a deep breath and told Paulie that everything was going to be all right.

"Daddy, how could anybody have come out to help us?"

"You'd better save your strength now," Kellan said.

"But Daddy."

"Paulie." It came out as a shout, but Kellan would explain later.

The boy lay quiet now. Kellan moved so that he might put his arm over him. He told him again that everything would be all right. Later, when they were on shore and the time was right, he would explain to him as best he could about his grandfather. And he would take back his lie about the dogs. The dogs were not special. He was old enough to know. Kellan's father had been right, and he would explain it all to him. For a moment Kellan lay resting with his head on his son's back.

In front of the boat, swimming and pulling, the painter's coil across his chest where it strained and cut, Kellan worked to bring the boat over the next swell. Though it wanted to go with him, the boat dragged against him in the troughs and he buried his face in the water to get his back into the pulling. When he could lift his head, he saw that they were less than two hundred feet out and that the fire on the beach was blazing higher against the trees. Kellan could pull them in, and it was past the time that the cold could take him.

He worked with the sea now, hauling and pulling harder toward the dark inland. With his eyes fixed on the fire, Kellan pulled against the weight behind him and against his own.

THE SOUND OF THE LAFAYETTE ESCADRILLE

It is early morning, night really, and I am in my father's arms with the cold of a Michigan autumn on my cheeks still warm from sleeping. He carries me carefully, wrapped in the quilt from my bed, and he walks sideways down icy steps to ensure his footing, and though I can't see it, I can hear and smell the car in the sharp cold, its motor running to prepare a warm place for me where my mother already sits, leaning sideways in the seat, her hand on his open door and waiting. Overhead, beyond the distant tips of pines in the yard, small failing stars throw a scant light through high thin clouds, and though I know she is there in the dark and waiting, I cannot see her and must rely on drowsy night senses to know my world. As we come down the porch steps, the car engine idles heavily at the end of the sidewalk and sends into the air the smell of exhaust. My father's arms draw me up and, to see his way safely, he lifts my head to his picky cheek and presses it there, breathing in my ear as he walks. Above me the roof of our house vaults into the night sky and high in the gable end a single night light, my room, blanches a light white square. Against the chill on my face and hair I call up a vision of my bed there, familiar, wrinkled, with a warm deep socket in its center, its quilt torn away and sheet trailing white on the floor, but then I am in the car and the vision blinks out like the end of a movie in the mild yellow of dashboard lights. She is there and I am with her, my chilled cheek newly warm in the deep curve of her lap and her voice comes to me through her stomach, wavery, as if from a long way off and through moving water. Pale in the dark (sweetly heavy with Jergens against chapping), her hand smooths the hair off my forehead and then he is there in the car with us ("All set?") and lifts my feet to settle them in his lap and grinds a gear ("Let it idle too long.") and then we are moving. In the backseat, leaning off to the corners against the windows, my two brothers, older than me, are drawn up under one blanket like a child's toys and lean into sleep again against the steady hum of motor and tires on the near bare pavement. The end of this ride will see two of us in bed again at Grandmother's while Father and Matt hunt for ducks in Merrill Lake, but for now, for an hour, it is the five of us against the night and I do not sleep but listen (myself a bridge joining those I love) to see if in their talk they will tell me what the threat of menace is I feel and whether or not the love we have for each other will bear it away.

For the moment, though, they are happy and I can feel their happiness through me like electricity through a wire. His hand rests on my ankle and circles its thin bones while her hand lies lightly on my head and ear and makes airy noises there like a seashell. He speaks to her in the voice he uses for grown-ups, as if we weren't there. "He's getting big. Long," and she answers, "Like Matt," (my oldest brother) and her hand goes away and with it her lap and she is busy behind the seat with their blanket and he says, "*It's* warm in here, Duch, they're okay," and then she is back again and he is saying that by the looks of us we will all be bigger than he is. Through her voice in her stomach that moves against my ear I can hear her smile as she says, "Good things come in small packages," and he smiles and says, "But not small altogether, I hope," and she says, "No, not altogether," and I know that she is smiling and he is and I don't know why. And I cannot imagine being bigger than him, though I know many men who are. When he turns his head to look at her, he is against the moving sky in the window and his hair makes a long *V* in the middle where his forehead goes up on either side and she reaches with her other hand to touch him there on that high crescent of skin. "How do you feel?" "Fine, good, we're going to get a break on the weather. They'll be up today." "You didn't get much sleep. I heard you up." "I'm fine, fine, really." And the throb of the motor in the floor moves us through the dark this night to another world.

We are going to Grandmother's. Each time I think it or hear it said, I see in my mind the grandmothers who are visited in the books in my school—little white-haired ladies who stand by wide, white board fences and wave to grandchildren who run by fields full of cows to greet her. The grandmothers in the books are always very small, with glasses, and wear their white hair wrapped in braids and somehow always manage to have ponies on their farms, and I am puzzled because I have never seen a grandmother or a farm that was ever truly like that. Nor cars like the hump-backed blue and red ones the families in the books go visiting in, and it bothers me because I am good on cars and know every make and model from 1930 on and know, too, that my father had to take good care of our 1940 Plymouth because none were made from 1942 to 1946 because of the war. As for my grandmother's farm, it is not a farm at all. There used to be animals there when my mother was a girl, but now there is only the house with a roof that slants four ways and a cement porch with my mother's initials in it. My uncle Eugene lives there too and is a sawmill superintendent for Henry Ford and has been since 1946, when Ford came to the Northern Peninsula to build mills to make lumber for the panels in the sides of his station wagons. Behind the house is a strawberry patch and a washhouse and between it and the edge of the woods is my mother's cousin's house, with squirrels in the eaves and broken windows and bird shit on the upstairs floors and, on the outside, brittle shaly paint that flicks off like scabs under my fingernail. It has been standing empty since the first of November in 1944, when my mother's cousin, who was angry because his windows were soaped the night before, declared that if it snowed that night as the radio predicted he was leaving for California at the first flake. That night he woke to go to the bathroom and, seeing snow on the ground, he woke his wife and told her that if she wanted a father for her children she had better wake them and start to pack. She did (wanted a father and packed) and they left town at five o'clock in the morning and they were gone for six days before he called anyone to let them know where they were. There is his house and behind it, in a clump of poplars with leaves that whistle in the summertime, is a stand-up safe as high as I am with a door that won't budge, which my mother's cousin bought to keep and sell for the metal and then could not get on a truck again once it had been dropped in his yard. Of him I share my father's opinion, because it is his: Say what you want, he is at least a man who made up his mind to do something and then went ahead and did it. Give him credit for that.

This morning my brother and I will wake there at my grandmother's house, where we have been put to bed again, and when we do it will be as if we have awakened in a new world. I will not walk downstairs to breakfast, but will walk flat out of her bedroom off the kitchen and sit down at her square table (ours at home is round) and will be given a choice of what I want for breakfast. If they are back from hunting, he will stand by our chairs and he will kid us about how our grandmother spoils us and how we will probably not want to go home with him when it is time to leave.

That will come later, though, and now they are talking again and I listen in the hope that maybe they will talk of what it is I fear and in the talking of it dispel it as he does the shapes in my room by leaving the light on. Maybe, too, at the end of this night he will say, "That better, Cowboy?" as he does standing in my doorway in his pajama bottoms, and the threat of menace will be gone. She talks first and in her voice there is something that says he doesn't have to answer if he doesn't want to. It says, *We can talk about something else if you would rather do that.*

"What do you think you'll say if he asks?"

"He probably will ask, won't he?" he says, and in the light from the dashboard his face has two points, his nose and his chin. Above, a line seems to pass over his eyes as if he were looking into a bright light. That look is in his eyes whenever they talk about the job Uncle Eugene has offered him at the mill and the look says he hurts. She does not say anything except, "Probably," and then later, "Maybe not, though," and then they are silent again and there is only the steady hum of the motor and the tires and the airy noises like a seashell in my ear under her hand. Soon, though, I am smiling at other noises, those in her stomach like mine makes in school in the morning and my smile turns my face and he sees me.

"You awake, Cowboy?"

"A little bit," I answer, and we have begun our game again.

"A little bit? Now, how can you be awake a little bit? You tell me what part is sleeping," and here his hand starts at my feet and tickles ("Here?") and then to my knees ("Here?") and then to my ribs ("Here?"), where this time he tickles until I cannot catch my breath from laughing and I hug his arm and she says the two of us are going to wake my brothers and that he is worse than the three of us put together, but smiles when she says it. I can hear her smile in her voice.

We are a *family* of games, mostly made-up games.

He makes them up. In the evening after supper, he lies stretched out on the couch in his work clothes with his head in her lap while with one hand she brushes his hair up and back, her hand rising and falling regularly as if she would put him to sleep. The games, like the faces he makes to amuse us, come to him as he lies with his head on her bare knee where her dress has slid up and he talks to us like that, his mouth moving on the curve of her knee and his hands tucked in against his belly. (In the summertime when he lies on the couch without a shirt he has another *V*, this one at his throat, the color of varnish, where the sun has gotten at him through his open collar and colored him, leaving the rest of him white except for his face and hands.) Like that, with his head on her knee, he will make up games for us, games of guessing, counting, finding, deciding, making them up, and the rules, on his fingers, which glide along on the rug in an effort to say, Do you see? then retreat to tuck in at his belly to wait with his eyes to see what our answer will be. And our answer is, "Yes, we do," which means, "Yes, we will," and against the call of playmates and the sweet rushing hours of playtime between supper and bed, the three of us play our game of playing at his, aware all the time of Mother's eyes above his head in hard entreaty, flinty in their resolve to stay us from leaving, saying silently to the three of us what she has never said aloud: "You are old enough to understand. You can do this much for him. Stay." And so we stay.

For that reason and because we have heard them talking, we stay. Upstairs at night where we lie on my bed, we have heard and seen them through the register talking below in the kitchen. My brothers and I have heard him come in at night and they have come down the short hall from their bedrooms to mine, where we take our positions over the floor register. Below, they are sitting at the kitchen table. She is sitting across from him with her hands stretched across the table to touch his hands and in her voice is a hardness toward us that we have only lately begun to hear. It is a strange tone, almost angry, which seems to put us outside their life, and through the register we watch them as if they are strangers. (The tone in her voice gives me the feeling I have had when, wakened by noises on another night, I walked downstairs and through the darkened rooms and saw him in the light from their bedroom door stepping naked across the hall to the bathroom.) This night he has been drinking again and we know she has waited up for him, waited sitting there at the kitchen table until he came home from the bars, those places downtown with names like Paradise, Tino's, Rainbow, and Pioneer, whose brightly colored fronts have fans that blow the warm smell of beer and peanuts and smoke into the street and that cannot be called because they have no number in the telephone book. She has waited up for him again this time, because when he comes home he will not feel well and he will say that he is no good. We know with her that he will say this and we don't know why, and in our beds, where we have not slept but have lain awake alone in our rooms, we have waited with her for him to come home so that from our secret perch upstairs we may somehow understand and maybe, in some miraculous way, will him to feel better. We do this because she has led us to believe that it is partly our fault. From our darkened room above them we watch and listen.

He calls her Duchess. He tells her that she shouldn't have waited up, that she should have gone to bed. He has a sickness in his mouth and eyes, and in our darkened room above them Matt says that he is drunker this time than ever before.

"It was getting late," she tells him. "I didn't know if you were all right." He cannot get his coat off and she helps him. "How do you feel?"

"Me? I'm fine. Nothing ever happens to me, Duchess. You know that. You shouldn't have waited up."

"I couldn't call. I was getting worried." Now she is touching his hands across the table. "If only I could call, I wouldn't be so worried."

"Worried? About what? Nothing ever happens to me, Duchess. I couldn't hurt myself if I tried. If I jumped in front of a train it would miss me. For anybody else it would be all over, but that train would grow wings and fly right over me. You ought to know that, Duchess."

"Yes, well okay now, but let's go to bed. You have to get up for eight o'clock."

"Don't you know that, Duchess? That old train would just grow wings and fly right over me. Caboose and all. Never touch me. Anybody else'd be cut in half. Not me. People like me, Duch, never get a scratch. We never get hurt."

"Stop talking like that and come to bed now. We'll talk about it tomorrow. Seven o'clock is going to come early."

"No, that's true, Duchess. We never get hurt. People like me never get hurt. You look at me, Duch, do I ever get hurt? I hurt *you* . . . and the *kids* . . . but I never get hurt. It's the way we're made. People like me."

"Okay, you never get hurt, but stop talking now. We'll talk about it tomorrow. You have to get up in the morning." She is half out of her chair now, pulling her bathrobe around her, but he does not get up. He sits in his chair and looks up at her and the sickness in his eyes makes him look as if he will cry. The light in the ceiling is yellow in his eye. "It's true, Duch, I know it and you know it. What do I do except drag you and the kids from one place to another? You can't even say. And now I'm talking about dragging you off again. My God, you *started* in Preston . . . . even your cousin had enough sense to make up his mind and stick to it. And he took his family *out* of this godforsaken country."

"There's nothing wrong with Preston. You like it. You like to fish and hunt . . ."

"Sure, *I* like it. It's always what *I* like. What about the kids? They like it here. What? . . ."

"Those kids have plenty. I've told you that. If you decide you want that job, those kids go where you go. That's all there is to it. You're their father . . ."

"I'm their father," he says, and a smile cuts his face. "Some father."

He means that we have lived in many places. He means that we have never had a home of our own, because he is never satisfied with his job or the town and we always move on to some other place. He means that my older brothers have lived in five different towns and I have lived in three and that we spend most of our time making new friends or saying goodbye to old ones. He means also that Preston, where Uncle Eugene has offered him the job in the mill, is a small town at the end of a road that runs along the shore of Lake Superior and then stops. The road does not go beyond Preston. In addition to Grandmother's house, Preston has one school, which goes to the eighth grade, a Protestant and a Catholic church, a store in a gas station, and a bar. In the town, the people call the bar a tavern. The town has three streets, which all lead to the mill, which sits on flat land below the hill on which the town is built. All around Preston are woods full of game, and though he loves to hunt in the winter and fish in the summer, he has told her that Preston is no place for boys to be raised and that if we are to do better than he has done, we must be brought up where there are better schools and more opportunity. He has said that if we do not do better than him, he will never forgive himself and that the reason we have moved so often is because he has had no skill or talent to trade on and has had to rely on luck. Our lives, he has told her, his boys' lives, must rely on luck as little as possible.

"Come here a minute." He slides away from the table and pats his leg for her to sit down. "Come here a minute. I want to ask you something."

"Lawrence, it's late. Can't it wait? We have to get up in the morning."

"Just for a minute." She comes around the table and halfway there he takes her hand and leads her to him. It is strange to see her on his lap, and for a moment I am reminded of the time I saw him stepping naked across the hall to the bathroom and I don't know if I should look, but then he asks her a question that takes us all by surprise. Her arms are around his neck, and when he asks, she sits back and looks at him and smiles. Her smile is like a little girl's. "When you were small, what did you want to be when you were big?"

"What?" Her eyes smile at him.

"What did you want to be when you grew up?"

"I don't know, Lawrence. What I am, I guess. A wife and a mother. Isn't that what all little girls want?"

"I don't know. I suppose. Do you know what I wanted to be? I bet you can't guess."

"No, I can't. Tell me."

"A flyer in the Lafayette Escadrille."

"What is *that*?"

"The Lafayette Escadrille. The American flyers who flew with the French in the First World War. Before we officially got into it. They just went over and volunteered and I'd read about them. I was just a kid then, but I've never forgotten how much I wanted to be one. They named their dogs Whiskey and Soda."

"Dogs?"

"Two of them. Whiskey and Soda. They had the life. I used to dream of flying with those guys. Jesus, I used to dream for hours. I had it all figured out how I'd get across someday and maybe lie about my age and once they gave me a plane I'd maybe never have to come down. Did you know that they used to grease the engines on the Nieport 17's with castor oil?"

"Lawrence, let's talk about it in the morning, okay? It's awfully late. C'mon now. You need your rest." She is standing now, pulling his hands. "C'mon, it's late."

"The Lafayette Escadrille. I *still* think about it. First, like all the other kids, I thought of the Foreign Legion and then one day I read about the Lafayette Escadrille. Just the sound of it. The Lafayette Escadrille. My whole life and I still think about it. At times I still think I'm going to join it. I find myself making plans, seeing myself in a uniform, and then I'm up there flying over the land and then lifting up to the clouds and down again. I still think about it, Duchess."

"Lawrence, it's late. Come to bed now."

"Do you see what you drew, Duch?" he asks her. She is standing holding his hands, but he does not get up. He only sits and looks up at her. "Do you see what you got saddled with?"

On these nights when we have waited up with her for him to come home, he does not go to bed with her when she goes. He sits alone in the kitchen and turns the radio dial to a station that plays music all night. When she leaves to go to bed, he turns out the light and sits beneath us in the orange glow of the radio dial. She calls him to come to bed and he answers that he will in a minute and that she should go to sleep. In a minute she calls softly to him again and he says that he will and he continues to sit there in the dark and then she is silent for a long time and the four of us know that she is sleeping and that she will not call to him again. Then there is only the dark and the round orange glow of the dial and the music, which swells and is clear and then fades away to become talk and air and at times becomes just noise as the night outside brings to the radio the confusion of three or four stations, which it plays at the same time. He does not change the station but only sits there in the dark in the glow of the radio dial and one by one we get up from our places and go to our beds.

Outside of our car the black shapes of trees against the blue-black of the sky flick past our windows, and their long silence has grown louder in the absence of a noise that can be heard only now, when it is no longer there. What we miss is a ticking that in our forgetfulness had run together like spokes in a wheel and had produced only a long *ting* which, once heard, disappeared. Ahead of me, on a level with my eyes, something else is missing and I am staring at the dead gray eye of a little bulb that glows red to show when the heater is on. The switch for the heater is below the bulb and the whole affair is tucked inconveniently under the dashboard. It has to be that way, because it is a heater from a junked 1938 Plymouth that he had to install and the wires were too short for him to hook up any other way. The day he put the heater in, he had lain across the front seat with both doors open with his head upside down on the floor and had proclaimed to my mother, who stood outside and handed him tools, that along with other talents he lacked, he had a conspicuous lack of talent for things mechanical. If it held up for a month after his hand had touched it, he said, then he would renew his faith in the existence of miracles. I pull the quilt higher up on my neck, and he sees me and listens and looks at the small dead bulb.

"Jesus, Duchess, did that heater just quit? See if you can try that switch. Can you reach it?" She is leaning down to reach and my head is caught between the bone in her leg and the softness of her chest. "Can you reach it? Jiggle it a little bit."

"I can reach it, but it won't go on."

"Did you try jiggling it? With luck, it's just a short in the switch itself." He is driving with one hand now and leaning over me to see under the dashboard. His one hand rests on top of the wheel and is the color of mustard in the light from the dashboard. His head is inches from my shoulder and then the steady hum of the wheels is broken and we are bouncing along on the shoulder of the road and she is screaming, "Lawrence," and he sits up and fights the car back onto the pavement again. The pavement is high and the tires scrape along its edge before lurching up over it.

"Jesus, that's good for the tires," he says, and then we are smoothly slowing down again and gradually we go off to the side of the road again and bumpily coast along on frozen sugar sand and gravel until we roll to a stop. His hands are shaking, and he folds them over the steering wheel and looks across and above me to her.

"I damn near *killed* all of you," he tells her. "I almost killed my family over a blitzed car heater."

"We're still alive, aren't we?" she says. In the backseat, Matt wakes to ask if we are there and she tells him almost and to go back to sleep. To him, she says that maybe we should just sit and rest for a minute.

"Rest? Duchess, I have to make a move. I have to do something. We've got thirty miles to go and you people are going to freeze. Look at him, bundled in there like he's dug a hole and pulled the top in over him."

"Lawrence, nobody got hurt," she tells him. "Now, we only have a little ways to go, so why don't we go on? The boys will be all right. Just rest for a minute and then we'll go on."

"What about you?"

"*I'm* all right. If I get cold I'll just pull his quilt up over me. It's not really *that* cold."

"It's cold enough."

"We'll *live,* Lawrence. Just rest for a minute and then we'll go. We don't want to wait too long or it'll be too late for you and Matt to go hunting."

He tells her then that he's not sure if he should go on to Preston at all and he puts his head down on his arms, which are folded across the steering wheel. She does not say anything except, "Rest for a minute," and then there is only the noise of the motor running. Outside, the blue-black of the sky is giving way to a purer blue and the stars, with the exception of one that I can still see, have gone out and have been replaced by faint wide streaks of white. Next to our car where we are parked on the side of the road a maple tree has become lighter and is no longer black. Its branches and trunk are now gray and a few dead leaves that did not fall the month before are rocking slightly in the early morning breeze. Her hand again is lying on my ear and, though I have never seen it, I can imagine the roar of the sea.

"It's just like me, Duchess. *God,* if it isn't."

"What's just like you?"

"To do what I'm doing."

"What are you doing? What are you talking about?"

"Look at me, Duchess. Here I am going off hunting as if I didn't have a care in the world and that man up there when he sees me is going to expect an answer. And he deserves an answer, Duch. Here he's doing me a favor and I act like he's put a curse on me. All he's done is offer me a job."

"Well, it's not even for sure that he'll ask, but if he does, just tell him that you want to think about it some more."

"Think about it? Duchess, look outside. Another week and we're going to get snow that's going to stay and then where'll we be? I'd have to get you people moved, pull the kids out of school. . . . Besides, he deserves an answer."

"Deserves?"

"Yes, *deserves.*"

"He's a saint?"

"He's an important man, Duchess, a superintendent. He's been put in *charge* of that mill and he's gone out of his way to offer me a job. The least I can do is tell him whether or not I'm going to take it. Don't you see that?"

"Gone out of his way? What is he now, Lawrence, a god? What I see is that my brother knows a good worker when he sees one and so he has offered you a job. Now, whatever you see in it, that's all I see. As for these kids, they won't melt."

"Duchess, wait a minute. Just wait a minute. How old is your brother?"

"How *old?*"

"How old is he? He's one year older than you, right? And what does he make in one year? Almost twice as much as me, right? Now, how old am I?"

"You're eighty-seven and you should be ashamed of yourself for snatching me from my mother's arms the way you did. Lawrence, if we're going to talk, let's talk on the way. You're not going to be able to go hunting at all. It's almost daylight."

Her hands slide under the quilt. She whispers to me for him to hear that there is a strange old man sitting next to her and do I think that we should run. She shrinks away from him, smiling, and then we agree that he looks harmless enough and that it might be nice to have him around for a few hundred years. He does not smile and so we quit. From the backseat, Matt says to turn the heater on.

"Duchess, all I'm saying is that your brother is a successful man and that from guys like me he deserves an answer. Do you know that in six months one out of three Ford wagons will have wood on its sides that has come from your brother's mill? Guys like him and even your cousin Dennis are miles ahead of guys like me."

"Dennis? What does he have to do with it? He's only miles *away.*"

"Say what you want. He made a move and stuck to it."

"Yes, and you're forgetting something, too. Eugene has never had a family to worry about, either. He hasn't raised three boys who will turn out to be good men like their father. You've forgotten all about that." She reaches to lay her hand on his cheek. He is still bent over the wheel, and like that, with his head down, he looks at me and smiles. Part of his smile is in his sleeve.

"You cold, Cowboy?"

I answer no and he reaches to pull the quilt up around me and around her and he says that I should hang on and that we will be home in less than an hour. My two brothers in the backseat, he says, are tougher because they've had to put up with him longer.

"Home? Lawrence, aren't you going on to Preston?"

"Duchess, I can't," he says, and something in his voice is angry and sad and she is angry too and she tells him that he is foolish and that we have come too far to turn back. I have never heard her say anything like that to him before and he tells her that he is not a fool but a failure and that the difference is something she should be aware of. He says that she should have been aware of it when she married him.

The return ride home is quiet. I am sitting up now, fully awake, while in the backseat my two brothers become more awake as the morning light washes into their eyes. Matt asks where we are going and she tells him *home* in a tired voice and the sound of her voice says *don't ask why.* He asks anyway and she says *ask your father,* which he does. My father calls him kid and says that of the three of us, he is the most unlucky because he is old enough to realize certain things about his father that must not be very pleasant for a kid of his age to think about.

Matt only grumbles and does not say anything more. Outside, the sky is round and low with flat gray clouds and it is as if their leaden heaviness has moved into the car with us and pressed us down into silence. Matt's disappointment is a presence in the car that crowds us and that we have to make room for. He is fourteen and has pointed out to my brother and me that our father only makes up the games and tries to amuse us with funny faces when he has been out drinking the night before. He speaks once more on the way home, to say that he never should have bought a license for all the hunting he is going to be able to do. My mother tells him to be quiet and after that we ride back toward town in silence. As we near the outskirts of town, the trees along the road begin to thin out and gradually give way to frost-covered fields that stretch back to old farmhouses and high bold barns with signs on their sides. Along the far edges of some fields are tall elm trees that stand like giant fans. Gradually, the farmlands give way to small knots of houses and roadside gas stations with barrels and old cars clustered around them. Some houses have dim lights burning in their windows and a few cars with squares of frost scraped from their windshields stand idling and warming up in driveways. It is cold in our car now, at times we can see our breath, and he says that if fate had in any way been fair, at least his family would be in one of those warm cars. None of us says anything, it is too cold to talk even for his sake, and as the clusters of houses become rows with street signs and still-lit street-lights, we shiver our way back into town, our only greeters a few town dogs and a sleepy milkman too busy to notice.

By the time we get home, it is snowing lightly and she says that it is too early to do anything so we go to our rooms and wait for the day to begin. Below my room he is rummaging through kitchen drawers looking for tools and he tells her that though there is no reason in the world to believe that it will last, he is going to try to fix the car heater again. She stands by the sink, her hands around my folded quilt, and though her face says she would say something to him, she does not and he pulls his collar up around his neck and plunges into the snow outside. As the outside door slams, she goes to the inner door and closes it and then crosses to the table and sits down. She is still holding my quilt in her arms and she lays her cheek against it and I turn away.

Beyond my window, the snow is falling in flat wide flakes and I watch him as he makes his way in the snow across the lawn to the car. Against the wide white of the lawn he looks hunched and small, and though I have watched and listened, I have not learned what it is that threatens us nor what has taken him so far away that not even our love can bring him back. Blowing on his hands and stamping his feet, he opens the car door and I ask of the silence in my room why it is that he cannot fly.

FIRST LIGHT

By now he is up and almost ready. In the dark he finds his clothes by feel and fits socks to feet and legs to pants and, sitting on the floor, searches with his hands until they touch his shoes and he pulls them on. None of it is as difficult as he thought it would be; simply a matter of letting your skin tell you when things are in their place. Then the shirt, a problem in the bad light, but only until your fingers convince you in their way that, right or wrong, you are buttoned up and what difference if you are one short on the bottom or one too many on top? If you are warm enough or as warm as can be expected, feel your way through the house with your hands on the walls of halls, past breathing bedrooms with their smells of heavy adult breath and bodies and bedclothes, past the brighter, gurgling bathroom and through the humming kitchen, to the porch cool and slippery, the early-morning moon a pale coin in a paling sky. And across the lawn in a slow hurry to be there on time, the lawn a moon-shadowed, rich slick of spring dew under foot, its green merely dark in this late light and no more green than the other no-color around, bush and tree, shed and garage—and hedge and car and back fence and kitchen garden—all to be found by feel and some sight in their cool dew and passed. And down the two-rut sugar-sand road to the mill, walking by feel the grassy crown in the middle, avoiding the grinching sand in the ruts to either side with its mind to turn an ankle or twist a knee.

To the mill. In the early light, its shops and sheds and storage buildings sit low against the dark trees behind. In the yard the rows of lumber piles squat squared and wet and dimly salmon-colored, imposing their shapes and stacked uniformity of row upon row on the irregular scene before him, a ragged, open patch of raw ground torn from the woods to make a sawmill, one of the three he has lived by in his nine years. Everything that matters depends on his being there on time, before the crew appears, the men who make the logs lumber and those who pile it into stacks as it comes out of the mill's other end. It is a matter of being there on time where no one can see him but he can see.

In place, hunkered down between the piles, he can only look up. The sky at this time of morning lifts lightly into itself, bluing into washes that climb, the whole lightening the woods' dark edges so that trees slowly accomplish, far tips against the paler blue down to thickening bodies to spread skirts lost in the ground's dark. Like that, neck chilled and cramped, new lumber's heavy sweetness in his nose like a cold, he waits.

A truck backfires up on the hill in the big garages. Another roars then grows calm in its even idling. In the mill a test saw screams then whines awhile and then is quiet. If it were a half-hour later, the saws would be going and he would just be waking, but that would mean that it was beyond the last few days in time, when he had seen and heard them and their loud talk and sometime shouts and doors slamming in the middle of the night. And then it would be even beyond then in time, when his older brother had begun saying that he was a man and *graduated* and for Christ's sake. . . . All of it would mean they were all back *then,* now seemingly long ago, when time was numbered by days in school, holidays, or so many weeks or months until one would end or another would come, that part of his life ever since he could remember when he had grown as naturally and without thought as the trees and bushes familiar to him in their places, his own progress marked by a single ceremony each fall when his mother measured him against marks on the bathroom wall just before school started again and wrote the numbers in a small book called *My School Years* which, she has told him, will be his to keep when he "goes." He cannot imagine "going" much farther than the mill or where the school bus takes him to, but his mother has said it and he has never known her to lie or to say something she didn't know was right, so he will wait and see about that too.

And he waits now. Waiting, he has learned, is a matter of putting your mind on something not connected to what you are waiting for, a trick. If he has understood what he heard through the floor register from the kitchen to his upstairs bedroom, it will happen here, on this lumber pile that his father and his piling crew have not finished putting into the railroad car. Whatever it is, it will happen here and maybe he will see it and understand as he does not understand their raised voices or, less, their silences, or the fact that his brother is as big as their father but is only one day out of high school and only half as old. If he can wait maybe he will see it, and so he puts his mind on something else (he settles on what there is to *see*) in order to trick it into coming.

The light that earlier had seemed to lift is now simply *here,* as if it arose from the ground itself, and surrounds him totally except where it makes small shadows thrown from the lumber piles, the standing railroad cars on the track, the trees at the woods' edge. Later in the day the men will call these shadows shade and go to it to sit or lie when they drink their coffee and have their middle-morning lunch. The light rises now with the ground's fine steam and warms him like the air in the kitchen when his mother washes clothes. Around him the lumber's resins pique his nose and clear it while up in the trees the birds he had heard small and singly in the dark have now started up their noises in full. The mill's noises, the saws and trucks and men, have with the light replaced the dark and cold and he waits damp and warming.

Above the saws he can hear men's voices as they come closer. He knows the men as his father knows them, by names other than the ones they were born with, and so of such importance as to sign them with mystery. There is Swede Erickson, with the big shoe, who used to drive one of the logging trucks until a year ago, when a chain pinched off his foot as easily, his father has told his mother, as you would a dead flower from its stalk. His father says that Swede is a good worker but that he drinks too much even for a man who has good reason. There is a man with a silly name, Tiny Bigger, who has a hole in his hair and seldom says anything. Another, one with a picture on his arm of a naked woman, which the boy would like to see better, curses a great deal and, his father has said, cannot be trusted to work his share. The fourth, an Indian whom the one with the picture on his arm calls Chief, is named Gus. He lives with his wife and many children in a shack by the edge of the woods where his grandfather sits on the door stoop all day and looks like he is sleeping behind the cigarette smoke in front of his brown face.

The men are closer now to where he sits and he can see as well as hear them. His father walks in front with his scaling rule and chalk marker and tally book. Behind him, the other men walk slower. Some are wearing their leather piling aprons and gloves while the one with the picture of the woman carries his as if he isn't ready to put them on yet. Swede tells him that he can't get any work done if he doesn't put them on and the other replies by saying something about the war and laughs in a way that seems to say that even though he is laughing, nothing is funny. His father doesn't say anything except to tell them that it's past eight o'clock and now they are on Mr. Yale's time and he cares nothing about who did and who did not fight in the war.

Up on the lumber pile the men step around and behind each other to pick up their boards after his father marks them with chalk and writes a number in his tally book. They are each dark against the sun behind them, and he closes his eyes and waits.

Yesterday, when he had seen his brother wearing a dress, he had not laughed because his brother had worn his look that said *don't* as he looked back at him in the mirror in their bedroom. When he had put on his hat, which looked like a board on a bowl, and played with its tail, the boy had felt the way he often had in church and left the room before it happened.

All that day, including the ride to the high school, where they saw his brother and all the others go up on the stage to get their diplomas, a "sheepskin," his uncle had called it, he had been with his family and relatives. They had given his brother presents and money and had all hugged him and the boy was glad that it was his brother and not him. Later there had been much pop and food and beer, and some of the older relatives played cards. His brother left then to be with his friends and the adults stayed and had a party of their own. His impression of the day had been one of standing at an adult's elbow or under their arm whenever it was impossible to get away. He didn't understand most of their talk and later, when they began to drink more and became louder, he understood it less but found it easier to sneak away as their grasp became looser and he could leave and they seemed not to notice. His uncle Bob later in the evening couldn't talk too clearly and mistakenly called him by his brother's name and gave him five dollars from the big bunch in his pocket he had made playing cards. He told him never to forget the last four years because whether he knew it or not, they had been the best ones of his life.

Later that night after everyone had left, he watched his father and mother through the floor register as they emptied plates and glasses and put dishes in the sink. His father was still drinking as he moved around the kitchen and his mother said, "Uh-huh," or nodded at the things he was saying. He was talking a great deal, mostly about the boy's brother, and was very excited. He spoke of "options" and "prospects" and "possibilities" and of the "future" coming, as if it were maybe something his brother would get in the mail like a package. He said in a voice the boy hadn't heard before that his brother had to be ready for it and that he had to be careful not to get off on the "wrong foot." That being so (the boy knew this by his mother's "uh-huh" as she rinsed dishes at the sink), his brother would never do as he did, step one foot into a lumberyard. The boy saw his father then as a younger man, the way he looked in the family photo albums in pictures taken long before the boy had been born, skinnier and with a pointier face, his hands deep in his pants pockets and usually leaning against a car or a tree. He saw his father taking a giant step onto a lumberyard and then changing sadly forever as if the ground itself were bad.

Just as he was about to get up and go to bed, his brother came in from being with his friends. Like his father, he had been drinking. The boy knew this because he had seen him drunk once before, when he had sneaked into their bedroom late one night and had given the boy fifty cents not to tell their parents. It hadn't been necessary to give the money. He would have kept silent for nothing in order for his brother to just like him more and tease him less, but he had been too weak to refuse. His brother had talked funny and then went straight to bed, where he had made curious noises and slept in a strange way, with one foot on the floor.

Now, his brother looked surprised to find his parents still awake and stood running his hands through his hair, which he seldom touched after he had spent a long time combing it to get it to go right. He moved around a great deal even though he was standing still and then he sat down hard on a kitchen chair. His father looked as if he was going to be mad but instead put his arm around him and said that it was a big day and that a man had to celebrate in the face of the future. His brother smiled at that and seemed to relax. He even moved his hand slowly, for all to see, toward a half-empty glass of beer on the table and took a sip. His mother looked at his father in her way, but his father only said that it was a special time, and he and his brother sat drinking and laughing about what they had done on their graduation nights. His father, they all learned, had helped take the four wheels off his principal's car and had piled them in the middle of the football field. His mother laughed but had said "Lawrence" in a way that said he shouldn't have. His father asked didn't she remember and she said that he had been too wild for her then. They both smiled at that.

Just then his brother got up as if to leave and the boy thought to go to bed before he was caught still up. Then his brother said something that made all of them be still. Mr. Yale, he said, had told him at graduation that he could go to work for him on Monday piling lumber in the yard. His father got up from where he was sitting and yelled that he would not. That he would never. Standing dressed up across from his father, his brother looked like him years ago in the pictures. His brother said that he was a man now and that Mr. Yale had said he could and that he was going to. That he could work as well as any man his father had on his crew and that he needed the money. That he was graduated and for Christ's sake. His mother got between them then.

"You're graduated? What the hell does that mean?"

his father said. "What do you know? One day out of school."

"Mr. Yale said I can."

"One day out of school and already you know. You haven't even returned the cap and gown yet."

"Lawrence," his mother said. "Let's talk about it in the morning. It's late."

"Maybe it's too late. Did you hear him?"

"Yes, I heard him. But let's go to bed now."

"You want to wind up like Swede, with a foot missing? Or Gus, who can't even feed a family and has to poach deer to keep their stomachs full? Or Meyers, who's probably just one step ahead of the law? You want to wind up like that?"

"What about you? You're a scaler," his brother said.

"It's the same thing. I have to work with them eight hours a day."

"You're not like them."

"And a prison guard's a guard, but he's locked up eight hours a day just the same."

"I didn't say I was going to stay there," his brother said.

"Neither were they, but they stayed, didn't they? Things happen. They didn't mean to get wives and kids and bills, but they did and now they're trapped."

"Lawrence," his mother said.

"One day out of school and already he knows."

"Lawrence, let's talk about it in the morning."

"You," his father said, and pointed at his brother. "You show up in that lumberyard and I'll see to it that you don't stay. I mean it."

"I need the money, and Mr. Yale said I can work. He owns the mill," his brother said, and headed for their bedroom. Against the sounds of a door slamming downstairs and his brother banging around in the bathroom, the boy went to bed and curled into himself against the wall. Later, when his brother was in bed and the house was quiet, he heard his mother call to his father to come to bed.

Sunday had been quiet. He went to church with his mother. When he and his mother arrived home, his father and brother were at the kitchen table drinking coffee, and something in their silence said that they had talked earlier and that now neither was saying anything. He had felt silences like that in the house before. Last summer, he had found a bees' nest in the bushes by his house. He gave his father and brother the same wide berth he had given the bees.

That afternoon his brother left again with his friends and didn't return until long after his mother and father were in bed. During the day, his father poured tomato juice into tall glasses of beer and knelt in their garden, where he drew lines in the dirt with his finger and stabbed seeds from bags into the ground.

His neck is stiff from leaning against the lumber pile and looking up. The men against the sky move the way people move in his dreams, slowly and as if they are pictures drawn under water. His eyes hurt, and he rubs them and waits. Up close as he is and with no house noises in between, it could be that the saws' screams are the men's as they lift the big boards and push them into the railroad car. Behind his father, they make faces and seem to like neither the boards nor each other.

Maybe he should have stayed home. Once, on his uncle's farm in Wisconsin where they had been visiting, he had gone into the barn on Sunday morning to see the mother cat's new kittens. The animals and the barn had seemed to be sleeping so early in the morning, and through the light from the dusty sun at the windows his uncle's arms had risen and fallen in the dim distance slowly and with care. As he had walked toward him down the long aisle, the pole in his uncle's hands had become a pitchfork and he saw that he was killing the kittens. While his back was still toward him, the boy had turned without saying anything and walked back out into the light. After church, at breakfast, his uncle had said in a loud voice to his father that he had given the kittens away to neighbors who didn't have any for their barns. The mother cat had sat on a square pile of hay looking down and washing her face with her paws.

Maybe he should have stayed home, he thinks again, but then his brother is standing before them all in the sand, a big leather apron over his shoulder the way the boy has seen pictures of bullfighters carrying their capes.

"Dad," his brother says.

"Matt," his father says, and puts down his markers and tally book.

"Mr. Yale said I can work in the yard."

"I know that. And I said you can't."

"I'm graduated."

"Yes you are," his father says, "but not to this." Turning to the men, he says, "You boys take a five. And a walk."

The one with the picture of the naked woman on his arm seems for a moment as if he won't move, but then his father looks at him *hard* and he goes with the others to climb down and walk a ways to sit against a railroad car farther up the track. His father says in a low voice, "Matt, don't come up here. Go home. Please."

"There's no work at home."

"There's none here either," his father says. "Not for you. You get a job in town. Work in a store. Learn a trade. Not in a sawmill."

"Stores don't pay," Matt says.

"This don't either. Not in the long run. Now go home. We'll talk there."

"We've already talked."

"Matt!" While his father stands with his hands on his hips, his brother climbs up on the lumber pile and then is facing him. His father only says, "Don't make me stop you."

When the blow comes, it seems to the boy's eyes motion without effort, the hand, that fast, then his brother turning in the air to lie curled tight on the sand. For a moment they had stood face to face above him not talking, the saws' screams seeming to say what no longer could be said, the distance between erased by the sun's brilliance so that for a split second there seemed to be not two but one: then they had separated by the movement leaving his brother holding himself on the sand. His father is speaking, "Now, go home." When his brother says nothing, his father says, "Goddamnit," and climbs down. His brother heads for home.

His father is standing around the corner of the lumber pile from where the boy sits. When his father had said, "Goddamnit," the boy had meant to leave, to get up and cut through the woods by the garages and go home after his brother. But his father is here now, too close, and he will have to wait again. He cannot see him. To be able to do that would be to reveal himself.

The sound he hears he has never heard before. It is an adult sound, wounded, and of such depth and anguish. There is in it something that signs the world of adults, which his brother is now entering and he will someday have to do. It is foreign, deep, and shows itself at times in their eyes when they talk of things he doesn't understand, the look he has seen upon entering a room unexpectedly and they have been talking. The look and the sound go together, but now there is only the sound and he tries not to hear it. He would have the saws drown it out, but his father is too close.

Then, against good judgment, he tends toward the corner of the lumber pile and looks around it slowly. His father is leaning there with his face in his hands. With whatever is in him shaking him and catching up his breath in such sounds, his father looks smaller and more alone than he has ever seen him to be. Turning and staying low, against the impulse to go to him, he leaves his father to himself and walks out of the lumberyard and goes home.

Inside the house, his mother is in the kitchen moving in her aproned ease from sink to stove to refrigerator and back again. His brother has left to be with his friends without her seeing him. The bruise high on his cheek had colored him there, and when they had met earlier in the day by the garden, his brother had covered it with his hand and walked by without saying anything.

Sitting on the porch, he is aware of the house behind him with its smells of cooking food and of the yard before him with a light wind moving high in the trees. The afternoon sun suspends and, whirling, spokes down through the tops of pines and the hardwoods' early leaves and into his small silence. In response to the hitting and his father's tears, his own tears start to come, but he pushes them back. He waits, thinking, *I am different now because of what I've seen. If the world stopped right now, I would go out of it changed because of what I saw and heard today.* In feelings not even loosely resembling language, he feels his sense of sureness slowly slip away. Its going makes itself known in his stomach as if a balloon were let loose there and is now rising to his throat. He has felt this before, the morning in his uncle's sun-dusty barn and once when his mother withdrew an inch-long sliver from his heel. The sensation was of being off balance, tipped, but each time he had righted himself and it had turned out that in the end he was okay. Though the picture of his uncle and the kittens stays in his mind, he can put other pictures around it that he likes and that soften it. As for the sliver, it is in a box in his room and now he can look at it without feeling the pain.

Though his mother tries to make both his father and him eat more at supper, they don't and his father leaves the table with food still on his plate. He would do the same, but his mother won't let him. When he finishes and goes outside, he sees his father standing in his garden but not doing anything other than looking into it.

He leaves him alone and cuts around the garage to where for the second time today he can see his father but his father cannot see him.

A tawny light lies off in the west, showing through the trees' small new leaves. In its pale bathing he thinks of the look on his brother's face and of his hand on the place where his father had hit him. And watching his father where he stands in the garden with his head bowed to whatever he is looking at, he hears again the sounds he had made from whatever place in his body they had been kept. Against them and in the name of whatever reason his father struck his brother, he squeezes down on this small resolve: that if the cause of what he has seen is love, then he will take pains in his life to never know anyone so well.

ROAD KILL

Looking back, I guess I had never liked Kessel much. We were partners in a car dealership, and on the floor, man for man, he outsold everybody in the shop. Legs wide, heavy-thighed, a mouth full of old gold, he went out to the showroom floor and a new customer like a young field officer going into his first battle. Most months he hung his own name and picture on the SALESMAN OF THE MONTH plaque in our office and he did it with a relish. When we came upon the deer at night on the way to a dealers' conference, he had been telling Owen, our bookkeeper, who was riding in the front seat with him, about an ugly Buick four-door he had sold to an old farm couple who had come in looking to buy a used pickup. He had sold them the Buick because it was an eyesore on the front line and he had simply not wanted it on the lot anymore.

Ahead of us in the headlights, kicking along the road's edge, pushing itself with its back legs while its one good front leg dug at the ground, was a deer, its head thrown up and back, its eyes rolling and yellow. The way it moved said that it had been hit by a car and broken up in the front quarters, the left side, so that the side flopped, moved differently than the rest of its body. At times three of its hooves just thrashed in the air until it could turn itself and dig into the ground and then it would move some more, inches, a foot, and then thrash again, scratching with its small hooves wherever it could get purchase, pausing there and pushing, stretching its back legs until they were out straight, then pawing with its one good front leg and moving some more. Under it and streaked through the white of its upturned belly, the blood from the gash behind its shoulder ran onto the roadside. In making its way, the deer had soaked up much of its blood in its fur so that its sides and haunches were liver-colored. When our car stopped, it rolled to its other side and when it did a piece of its shoulder bone slid white through its fur and stuck up and did not move when the shoulder moved. When it thrashed again, the bone moved back into its fur and then came out again, this time in a different place, where it tore the fur higher up on its neck. When the deer turned over again in its attempts to push, the bone disappeared and then slipped out again from its first place, lower down, and stood up white and streaked with blood. The deer moved independently of it and continued to try and thrash its way.

When we got out of the car, we could hear the small noises it was making. They were faint, liquid, mewling sounds and blood leaked back along its lips and throat. When we stood next to it, it lay with its one good front hoof in the air, pawing, looking up at us. Behind us the car idled in the dark. Except for our headlights, there was nothing to see but the deer—only it and its shoulder bone the size of a playing card white in the lights. I backed along the fender of the car and stopped with my hand on the windshield.

Staring up at us, the deer's eyes were unavoidable. As I looked at them they seemed to say *what?* and *why?* and made me think *what now?* I said it out loud, and Kessel turned to look back at me with a frown. Owen was out of the car too and had come around to my side to stand by me. We were on a long stretch of road in northern Michigan and we hadn't passed a town or a state-police post in miles. The road ahead of us didn't promise anything better. There were no houses and no phones. And we couldn't very well put the deer in the car. The car was one of this year's demos and we had plans to put it back on the lot and sell it after this trip. It only had eleven hundred miles on it.

"What do you mean, *what now,*" Kessel said, his back turned to me again. He was a big man, and bulking in his loud sports coat over the deer, he could have been a caveman squatting down to a fresh kill. "We're going to take care of it," he said.

"Take care of it?" I said. "Cal, there's no way . . ."

"Put it out of its misery," he said, squinting into the lights.

"Cal," Owen said. "Let's just . . ."

"How?" I said. I didn't like this whole conversation. I didn't like being stopped on this abandoned stretch of road with nothing but dark woods around and I didn't like this deer and its misery and I hated the person who had hit it and left it here for us to deal with. And at the moment I especially didn't like Kessel. He was an ass. A bore. He cared less about money than making the sale. That was everything to him, whether it was selling a gas-guzzling gunboat of a Buick to an old farm couple who had come in to buy a little pickup or simply outselling some new kid in his first suit on the floor, just to show him *who was who* in the shop. And now, hunkered down in his carny barker's notion of style in clothes, speaking in his matter-of-fact don't-you-know tone, I liked him even less, if that was possible. What I also didn't like about him was that our business did as well as it did because of his savvy and aggressiveness. "Couldn't we just slide it off the road and into the woods?" I said. "It's going to die anyway and it doesn't look like it's going to take long."

"Yeah," Owen said. "Let's just roll it off into the woods. Anybody can see that . . ."

"Not long for us maybe," Kessel said, "but then we're not doing the dying. If he suffers through till morning, the crows will take his eyes out before he's dead. . . . Christ. Look, do you guys want to just go sit in the car?" He looked at us as if we were less than some dumb customers.

After a long time with my hand on the car's warm hood and listening to its idling in the night, I turned to see Owen staring at me. Against the black to either side of the car behind the headlights, his shirtfront cut a pale white. His eyes locked mine for a second and then he retreated back along the car's length and let himself into the backseat and closed the door. Ahead of me, Kessel and the deer were locked into the shaft of light on the road, and I stepped up next to them. "What?" I said.

"Get me the lug wrench out of the trunk," Kessel said.

"The lug wrench?" I said.

"Yeah, the lug wrench."

"Why?" I said.

"Jesus Christ, Gene. Will you just get it? And after that you can go join Owen in the car if you don't want to be here. I don't want to be here all night, either."

My first impulse was to back away. At home I left these matters to Joan. Slivers. Pulling baby teeth, taking the kids to get their shots. What she and I both knew, that it had to be done and was for the kids' own good, was to her an unarguable fact that wiped out emotion as she gripped a baby tooth that was crowding a permanent one or sterilized a needle with a match and slid it into a finger or a palm of a hand. I had always wondered how she could do that and then was left to wonder again when later I saw that the child was no worse for wear and had indeed survived it. Added to that was the sensation that somehow the child and Joan were closer together after it was over and that I, somehow, was left out. When I returned to the room, the child was usually there with a treat of some sort, ice cream or candy, and holding the tooth or sliver like a trophy and smiling. Each time, I had promised myself that I would do it the next time. But the time had never come and my kids had had their second teeth for years.

"Gene, for Christ's sake," Kessel said.

"All right," I said. "All right. I have to get the keys."

"Then get 'em. But leave the lights on. They can kick like mules when they're down, and I don't relish getting my ribs stove in." The deer lay panting under Kessel's hand, where it spread just below its throat.

From inside the car, when I reached in to get the keys, Owen said nothing.

Back at the trunk, I moved luggage around and stacked some of it on the road to get to the spare-tire compartment. By feel I found the lug wrench behind the spare tire and slid it out.

In front of the car Kessel knelt by the deer at arm's length, with one hand still on its chest and his body arched away from its hooves. The deer was rolled up high on one side and its nostrils were wide with blood bubbling in them. Its chest heaved and made noises. In its one good foreleg I noticed another bone the size of a ballpoint poking through. I stood with the lug wrench in my hand waiting on Kessel.

"Well, for Christ's sake?" he said.

"What do you want me to do," I said, and stepped closer.

"Me and this deer don't have all night," he said. "Get over here and hold him like I'm doing. Hold him like this and watch his feet. If I can help it, I only want to have to hit him once. You got it?"

"I'll try," I said.

"You're going to have to do more than try, because if I have to hit him more than once, it's going to get messy. There, like that. Push down on his chest and his good shoulder. Stay forward of those back legs and watch 'em. If he twists so that he can get a crack at either one of us, it could be bad news. You want to get ready on this now?"

A light wind wandering low over the road brought the smell of warm blood up to my face as I squatted without kneeling by the deer's side and tried to place myself and my hands as Kessel had told me to. The deer's body warmth and movement shocked me and I thought that I might get sick. Kessel knelt across from me in a crouch over the deer with the lug wrench gripped by the long end in his hand. For the first time I could sense the true power in his body. He tensed himself, setting the balls of his feet squarely under his body and adjusting his knees so that he could lift up on them and still be over the deer while keeping his balance. In my mind I felt Owen in the car, in the dark, behind the lights, watching. Kessel looked at me to see if I was ready. I pushed down on the balls of my feet and the palms of my hands. I nodded and looked off into the woods. To my blind side I could feel Kessel tense again, rise up and, after a moment, strike.

With my eyes turned away I had sensed Kessel's movement and anticipated the blow. Involuntarily, I had turned away. Freed on that side, out from under the pressure of my hands, the deer had felt space and had twisted toward it, his back legs digging, the strong push moving him a half a foot. The blow had landed low on his nose. "Son of a bitch. Goddamnit, Gene. I said hold him. Jesus Christ." The deer was squealing in pain, making noises I didn't know deer could make. A fine mist of blood hung in the air and settled damp on anything it touched. Against the pain, the deer's back legs scissored on the ground and it twisted its head over its shoulder, away from where the blow had come. Kessel, with a hard look at me, jerked its head back toward him and with a widespread hand forced its muzzle down. The deer's eye showed through his fingers. I found my place on the deer's chest and shoulder and pushed down. This time I looked straight ahead at Kessel's tie as he set himself again and rose up with the wrench.

At the sound (I had closed my eyes), I felt the blow and the deer quiver. At the same time I turned and lost my stomach behind its rump as its whole body stiffened to finally settle down under my weight. Where I was being sick, a dark urine lined with blood slowly leaked out into the ground. I got up from him and leaned on the hood. It was warm, too, and I walked away to stand off on the woods side of the car. "Goddamnit," Kessel said. "Blood and piss all over. All over my pants." For a moment there was just the car's quiet idling to hear and my own sickness to smell. The sensation was that it was over, then Kessel slammed the lug wrench to the road and I heard it bounce into the brush. "Goddamn animal," he said, and walked out of the lights and up the road by himself. I used my handkerchief to clean my face and hands and threw it into the woods.

In the car, Owen still sat in the backseat. I saw him briefly under the dome light, then I slid into the front passenger seat and closed the door. For a full minute it was quiet and I sat staring into the headlights' slice up the road. Kessel wasn't back yet and I was glad.

"So what'd you do?"

"You saw," I said. Owen's voice was small and I didn't want to hear it. I didn't want to talk to him. Especially now, I didn't want to talk to him. "Where'd he go," he said.

"I don't know," I said. "To hell maybe."

"Do you think he enjoyed that?"

"What do you think?" I said. After a while I slipped the key into the ignition and turned the radio on. Rock music blared out of it and I turned it down.

"What's the matter with you?" Owen said.

"Nothing's the matter with me," I said.

"I couldn't stay out there," he said. "I just couldn't do it."

"Yeah," I said.

"Where's the deer now?"

"Where do you think it is? Right where it always was."

"You didn't drag it off to the side?"

"No, and we didn't give it a goddamn twenty-one-gun salute, either. Did you? Do you want to?"

"Gene, you don't have to take this out on me. Why doesn't he come back so we can get out of here?"

"Good question," I said. My tone said that I didn't want to talk, and Owen read it right and shut up. After we listened to almost a full song on the radio, he started talking again in a low voice. I could barely hear him. "Did he suffer," he said.

"Who?" I said. "Kessel out there? That deer? Let's say that it was you that . . ."

"Gene, now you look. You know I don't want to hear . . ."

"No, you look. What the hell do you think this's been all about?"

After a while Kessel came walking down the road toward the car. His pants were stained dark where, we later learned, he had scrubbed at the blood and mess in a creek that crossed the road ahead of us. His tie was gone. He walked slowly toward the car and then turned to kneel by the deer. He knelt there for a few minutes with his head down. When he stood up with the deer's hind legs in his hands, Kessel's eyes were wet. He was dragging the deer backward toward the woods when I got out of the car. My own sickness was still heavy on the air. I heard Owen get out behind me.

"Cal," I said. "Just a minute, I'll give you a hand."

"No, I got him. There's not much to him," he said, and continued to drag him over the road's shoulder and then off into the woods a few feet. In a minute or so he came back toward the car brushing at his clothes and then we could hear and feel him at the trunk putting the luggage back that I had forgotten. He slammed the trunk door.

Back in the car again, he took the wheel and we were on our way. I didn't feel like talking, so I left the radio on and leaned back in the seat. Kessel reached and turned it down. His voice boomed. "I hope one of you guys has a tie you can lend me," he said. "And something else."

"What's that?" Owen said.

"One of you tell me a joke, the rottenest, most filthiest one you know. Make it one with some naked nuns and a bishop in it. Something with a sleazy motel and booze bottles all over."

"And mirrors on the ceiling," Owen said. "And a Magic Fingers bed."

"Sure, Owen," Kessel said, "whatever," and turned the radio up and drove with both hands on the wheel. At a speed way over the posted limit the deer faded behind us, into the woods, into the night, and into the past. Once I looked over at Kessel and his eyes were still damp and shining in the dull glow of the dash lights. My own were dry and my face felt tight. Sitting in the darkness, I determined that at this year's conference I would split off from him and Owen, move around more, make a point of meeting new people.

FOX FEED

"He had not thought about shooting the horses," she said. She went on to say again this night that it had never occurred to him that he would have to, would have to buy up old horses from around the county and lead them into the tall pens he had built into the woods a few hundred feet behind the house and, there, shoot them so that the fox could feed on fresh blood and flesh that would produce the pelts the furriers would buy. He had told her, she said, as if telling her would somehow make it all right, that the horses were going to be eventually sold and killed to make soap or glue or mink feed and at least his way they would be killed with one clean shot through the head and not beaten to death with a mallet in someone's back-alley slaughterhouse. "So" she said, "he said he would try . . ."

Her voice, Grandmother's, died away into the darkness beyond the half-circle of light shining into the yard by the light over the front-porch door. She insisted on still living here in the house that Grandfather had built for her, and so on summer nights like these my wife and I would drive the thirty miles from the city to this little town where she had lived sixty-seven of her eighty-one years. In this house she had raised her children and eventually outlived them—and finally her husband, too. My wife and I had to drive to her house at least once a week to check on her old stoves and rusted water pipes and to see, in general, how she was doing. After a brief check of the house, during which she insisted that she was fine and didn't need anything, we would go out to the porch before leaving for home and get the breeze where she would lightly lift and fan her apron dry and then spread it across her lap, arranging it over her knees and the edges of the wooden kitchen chair that she would not let me carry to the porch for her. Like that, her apron dry and smoothed down over her bent legs standing high at the knee and rising straight up out of shoes as high and rigid as a man's, she took up again the story she had taken to telling us during our last visits, about Grampa Perry and the fox and his not being able to shoot the horses. From within the porch light's overhead halo, her face jutting up against the town's dimmer halo wreathing the sky and her voice, high on old age, riding the warm rising currents of family history, she shaped in the air again the images that during the last months she had made ours, and so the three of us went back again through her sixty-seven years of living here in this same house on property that had held at one time three houses, where she and her sisters and their husbands had lived and where she had outlived all of them and most of their children and even her own three and now lived on through the gap left by her children's deaths to spill over into ours, her grandchildren's lives.

"So he said he would try," she went on. Her voice barely carried to the porch light's half-circle beyond which, to the back of the house, lay the remains of the fox pens ranging a quarter-mile into the woods where, tangled in the overgrown blackberry and giant Lombardy and pine whips, were the rib cages and skulls of a dozen or more horses, the last of which had been shot in mid-July of 1933. "He went out with his pickup on the first day and later in the afternoon came back with one, a big mare, black and swaybacked, that lumbered down off the truck and started cropping grass around the back tires and only once in a while looked off to the pens at the fox, as if maybe they were her friends. She just stood there swishing flies with her tail, and Perry petting and rubbing her mane looking across her neck at me and saying, 'There, there,' into her ear as if she knew what was coming. Then, when I didn't say anything, he picked up her bridle as if it were a snake and jerked her around. 'Get my rifle,' he yelled, and waited while I went into the shed and came back with it. 'Now go in the house,' he said, and walked off with her toward the big gate that led to the back of the pens. Ten minutes later I heard the shot, and then I heard him in the shed putting the gun away and then he came on through the kitchen and went on into the bedroom and closed the door. "That was the first one," she said, "and in a year's time there would be ten or eleven more and in that time he would start to change and none of us, not even him or me or your father, for that matter, would see it for at least another few years and by that time it would be too late."

The story didn't end here, only her voice. For a moment, with the night air weightless, the three of us sat listening to the random crickets spaced in the grass and, further back in the pen by the creek, the bass squawks of frogs. Down in the town, intermittent car horns blew to one another and then were quiet.

"The last time," her voice started again, high and unavoidable, riding the night air, "it was a bay stallion. In between it had been others, some of them pleasure horses, one of them an old Shetland that tourists had used to pull a cutter for their children when the Jensens"—a name we didn't know; she had lately taken to speaking of old people, her contemporaries, whom she assumed we knew—"used to rent their lake cabins and the tourists would come up from the cities for the ice fishing and the hunting and to use the cabins for Christmas with the trees and snow that they couldn't get in the cities. But mostly they had been work horses used in the woods for skidding timber, with some of them having been farm animals from up on the Keweenaw, where they had the potato farms. This one was a big, worn-out bay that twitched like a colt as Perry backed down off the truck and slipped an old towel for blinders on him so he couldn't see the fox who, since the first one a year ago, had taken to crawling out of their hutches or, if they were outside, just stopping and staring with their little slit eyes whenever one was brought in the yard. Behind Perry and the bay they made little noises in their throats that kept the bay's legs going like there were flies after them, and Perry petted him like all the rest and said, 'There, there,' and looked across his back at me and told me for the dozenth time to get the gun from the shed. I did, and when I came back, he was still standing there petting the bay and working his hand into its mane like he would tie it into knots. He didn't even look around at me when I handed him the gun, but just turned the bay easy and led him with that towel blinder still on down the path between the trees and into the pens. Once, I saw the bay pull back and stop, but Perry talked to him and petted him and then the bay moved again, following Perry down the path until the leaves got too thick and I couldn't see them anymore. I waited for a minute and then went in the house and sat at the table and waited for the shot and for Perry to come back. When after a half-hour I didn't hear the shot, I went out and sat at the picnic table under the trees and waited another half hour and still no shot, and then I saw Perry back under the trees coming along the path holding the gun by the barrel with the bolt thrown back, and with the other hand he was leading the bay, that towel blinder still on, trying to crop at the wild blackberry alongside. When Perry saw me, he didn't stop but went on past me and slapped and poked at the bay's hind end and got him up the ramp and back into the truck. When he had slammed the gate shut, he walked over to me with his eyes down and stood stock-still in front of me. 'I can't do it,' he said. 'No more horses. I can't shoot any more horses. I'm selling.' Two weeks later a company from outstate came that fast and loaded the fox and what feed was left and the hutches and as much wire as they could pull down into three big trucks and hauled the whole thing away. When they left, they gave me the check and the papers to sign because he would not come out of the house."

Then again she was quiet. Behind us, the house, and the woods beyond, the sky's early-evening dark was split with shafts of red and darker liver. Against it, in the thin light from overhead, her skin had the look of old varnish, as if over the years the sun and wind and equal time over stoves and space heaters had given her face the qualities of a found stone brought indoors and polished. Only in her eyes, dark in the yellow, was the vision alive, which tonight, in spite of all past failures, my wife and I were to see. My wife's eyes began to grow wide in the dark as if the silence had been too long, as if before us and in spite of everything, this night Grandma would die here on the porch and we would be faced with the funeral. For a moment we looked at each other in the lapse of her silence until her voice, unearthed, went on again. Behind us, the silence of the pens and their yellow bones crowded us even here in the open night air. "He was too young," she said. "A boy. Too young to do what he had to do."

"Had to do?" I said. "I thought it was his choice."

"There's a difference? He was a boy."

"Right," I said. "And he had to do this."

"The fox were supposed to do it. And so he built the pens. Just like the mill. In 1932 they were supposed to do it. That's all it would take. Those fox and a year of work and then your father's Aunt Stell and Uncle Ken and the others, they'd all be back here. That's all it would take. He'd make the one trip, get the fox, come back here, and in a year we'd have the money. A year, he thought. One year and then all his family, his family's family, to him it was all the same, would be back here from the cities where they went when the Depression came. That's all he knew. And the fox would do it. One year and they'd all be back. And when he couldn't do it, shoot the horses, that was the start."

"What did he do?" This from my wife, sitting at Grandmother's feet, her face in semidarkness at the light's edge. Her eyes had gone dimly out of focus in the way of someone being told a story.

"For a while, a month maybe, nothing. Nothing but walk out into what was left of the pens for hours at a time and switch around under the trees in the stink of fox droppings and piss and what meat was left turning bad on those horse bones. Sometimes I'd go with him and he wouldn't say anything but just keep moving slow from one to another. He'd find them where he had shot them, their big ribs and heads and legs a yellow against the leaves and ground and always that hole where he had shot them behind the ear. Sometimes two. Some of them with two holes where he had had to shoot them twice, because the first shot wasn't enough. The last one, the one before the bay, was the Jensens' Shetland, a puny thing, no bigger than an outsized dog, and it still had some of its hair on it and was all torn where the fox had ripped at it and torn out the insides. He'd stand there in the stink with his head down, too tired to even yell at the crows up in the trees who had taken out the eyes and were waiting for us to leave so they could light on the Shetland again. He'd just stand there in the pens in what wire was left hanging from the trees and those crows and those horses and wouldn't talk, and when he got like that, I'd leave and come back to the house because there was no talking to him. When he did come back maybe hours later he'd go to the bedroom, and I'd know he wasn't coming out. Then in the mornings he'd be up and out by first light and in those pens again. That went on for about a month."

"And then it was the mill," I said. We had heard the story before, never all of a piece, never in the weighted insistence of her voice tonight, but it was late and I was ready to head home. The rest of the story was for us in the old photographs in the shoeboxes in her cedar chest, piecemeal, out of time and order, black on gray on white, in crescent-shaped piles three to a box, curling over the litter on the boxes' bottoms of campaign buttons, watch fobs, and pale button hooks and cheap jewelry. Long before she had taken to telling us the story, in the last year or so, the photographs had given it to us in faces diamond-bright against the black of tar-paper shacks, those early hillbilly slums against the woods beyond, which, down through the illusionary twenties and hopeful thirties, were built, added on to, shored up, and pinned to cement foundations to appear in the forties to us, her grandchildren, with all the density and permanence of history and the woods themselves. Beyond those years and the houses that had come to stand for them (now, to either side, the houses gone, was a house trailer, the land rented out to pay the taxes on the property), there was nothing but an occasional reference over the years, and these from her, of her parents' and grandparents' names, dim, harshly biblical, redolent of cedar, where the Bible was kept in the chest with its register of family names. We had heard it before and were ready to be on our way home. Once she had told us of the mill again, we'd be headed back to the city and a drink and bed.

"So then it was the sawmill in the thirties," I said again. She hadn't spoken. "And he couldn't make those kinds of decisions. He was compassionate, Gram, human. You people had feelings, something rare today that you gave to all of us. You can be proud." In the next five minutes I saw Grampa Perry scrounge the materials, build, run, and fail to keep the mill and the family from going under. The whole of it, storyteller that she was once she had captured her audience, would be in the auto trip made in 1934, the family's famous trip with her and my father and him as the lead characters that I had heard at least a dozen times and my wife half that many. Between where we sat on the porch beneath and to either side of her chair, she sat above us, face shining like worn leather, temples cupped like anvil hammerings, and looked out over the town she would not leave.

Primed now with the mention of the lumber mill, she would tell it again, tell of Grampa Perry's building the mill by hand (that ruined building, too, stood graying into the woods beyond the house), but once started, would change direction, circle, and land on the auto trip in 1934, which to her had come to stand for the second disastrous decade, the gray but hopeful thirties, in images particular and emblematic. She had told us before and in telling us had made the images ours, so that now, as we sat and listened to her voice while waiting for it to end, we authored the story for ourselves, moving among the characters who were both familiar and strange. Though we heard her voice riding above us we did not listen to it, but instead saw it for ourselves, saw that *morning:* in the east the sun only a ragged lightened line against the blanched sky and that fact, the total lack of color, says that this June day is going to be hot and still. But that will come later. Now, at this early hour, it is just daylight, Lake Superior is still and near white and there is a hint of last night's cool and dew still in the air. Their children, with the exception of my father, who leans over the cab of his father's pickup preening into the wind, are huddled with their backs to the back of the cab trying to stay warm. For some reason that they don't understand, they are still in their pajamas and these stick out from under their coats, into which they have tried to get everything, arms, legs, and as much neck as possible, for this unexplainable early-morning ride from the hotel in the town they had visited with their father where he had gone to see about mill business. Their brother, the one who is standing and who doesn't know either why he is still in his pajamas, leans his face into the wind like a setter on point and, without looking down at either of them, tells them that they are both afraid, it's not cold and to try it. Either because of the clatter and whine of the old truck being so loud that they truly don't hear him or because they choose to ignore the bragging of an older brother who must be freezing to prove a point they consider pointless, they don't answer. They only huddle deeper into their coats and bury their eyes and ears against the chilling speed and noise. Since he cannot find their eyes and they refuse to listen, my father, the one in the wind, pounds on the top of the cab telling his father to floor it and why does he go so slow. Through the rear window he can see over his father's shoulder that they are doing sixty-five and even he knows that that is much too fast for this road that has killed half a dozen in his own lifetime and more that he has heard about, and so he wonders about that. And then says into the wind in his mouth, the hell with it, and pounds on top of the old pickup cab, telling his father to pour the coals to her.

Inside, Grampa Perry fights the play in the wheel and the looks from her, who lies huddled in the far corner, not from cold because it is warm in the cab, but in a still determination not to say anything about the speed, the hour, or the children in the back still in their pajamas and no food in their stomachs. He looks at her and wishes that he could say something to the unanswered and for that matter unasked question that crowds them in the cab, but can't and so he fixes on the road trying, by the concentration in his eyes and the working of his jaws, to straighten out the road and settle the loose wheel by force. Overhead there is a pounding, and above that and the laboring old truck his oldest son, a gawky boy of sixteen, is shouting something to him that he can't make out. Leaning out the window he shouts straight ahead into the wind for the boy to shut up and sit down and in the rearview mirror sees the boy slink down and join his brother and sister, whose heads are just visible in the window. Then his eyes come back to the road and stay there.

Judging from the few glimpses of the lake that they were now getting through the hardwoods on the ridges, he calculates that he must have about twelve miles to go. He has never figured it out in terms of miles before, because there had never been any need. Now, however, he knows he is coming up to Riggs' corner in a few minutes and then about two miles of straight road to Hair Pin curve and then about a mile and a half to Sun Lake and then about another two to the parking lot of Meyer's Mountain and another mile and a half to Stony Creek and then about four miles to town and home. Knowing he has the mile to Riggs' corner of fairly straight road, he pushes it to an even seventy and holds it there. In a minute he will have to back off, but then he will have two miles along the lake to come back to seventy and make time. But at seventy she shimmies so bad he worries about the tie rods and so drops it back to sixty-seven, where it quiets down, and he holds it there. Over the lake the sun is becoming less of a bright line and more of a ball and his watch tells him that he can slow down, he has an hour, but he doesn't. Can't. But he'll try about sixty-five, no, sixty-seven, and hold it there. Riggs'; he has to slow down.

In the slow and quiet of the corner the question comes. When he hears it he knows that that too has been one of the reasons for the speed, the urgency, as if somehow he went as fast as the truck would go he could get there on time and at the same time, with the same speed, head off the unanswered question before it was even asked. Up until now her quiet, hurt anger has held back the question all through being awakened from a warm and deep sleep, through a waking of the children against their mumbled protests, and a useless quiet shuffling of them still in their pajamas and half-asleep down hotel porch steps and across the still-moonlit yard and into the back of the pickup. She hasn't said anything up until now. For eighteen miles she has just slouched in the corner with her feet pulled up under her the same way she sits on the couch in the evening knitting or crocheting while she listens to the radio. Except that at home it is relaxing to see her sitting like that. Now there is something uneasy about her feet pulled up under her like that at five-thirty in the morning between fifty and seventy miles an hour.

"For what?" she says. "Kill us all for what?"

"Nobody's gettin' killed."

"So far." Fear and anger have flattened her voice.

"So far nothin'. We've done the worst part. I don't want to argue with you and I ain't," he says.

"Or talk neither, I suppose. We all get killed, the children still in their pajamas at daylight, and you can't find the time to say that the reason is a man who has never done a thing for you. For us."

"I don't want to argue," he says, "and I ain't. Soon's we get home, I'll get the children back in their beds."

"That's the best thing for pneumonia."

"I ain't going to argue, Lil. I got enough."

"Yes you do."

"Lil."

"All right."

"All right now." His last remarks are soft, conciliatory, an attempt to ease the harshness from her shouted name. Past Riggs' he brings it back to sixty-eight and holds it there. To his left, through the tin-colored maples the lake is coming up from near white to a pale blue and flashes at them. About nine more miles. Ahead, he can see the first leg of Hair Pin curve and he cuts it back to fifty-five, knowing that in a minute he'll have to take it all the way down to thirty or thirty-five at the most to make the curve. Into the curve at thirty-five he can feel that it is too much and so he brakes to thirty and by the time he comes out of the far side of the curve he is down to not much more than twenty miles an hour. He will be at Sun Lake before he is near seventy again, and then he will have to slow down again for the two miles of hilly curves that snake around the backside of Meyer's Mountain. From there the last four miles or so to town are peppered with houses, and even at this hour he will have to go slow for fear of hitting someone out walking. He will have to slow down from here on in. He'll hold it at fifty. Fifty-five.

Meyer's Mountain. Quarter to six.

"Is this it now? You going to settle down? Your watch say you got time to have breakfast before you rush out and try to save their lives?"

"I didn't mean to holler, Lil."

"I know. Ten minutes we'll be home."

"It's that it came to me during the night that what with that business yesterday, with the orders not coming in, I'm going to have to let Tom Farrell and his boys go. Maybe even some of the others, eventually. And I can't tell them at the mill."

"I know."

"They got to be told at home, where their people are with them. They're going to need them."

"They'll be there and you'll tell them and they'll get through it. Others have. We have."

Four miles at just under fifty-seven and then they are home.

He pulls up to the door of the house and goes around to get the children out of the back. His oldest, my father, who is wide awake from standing in the wind, asks him what their fastest speed had been, and he tells him "too fast" and to go in and to bed. The other two don't have to be told. They climb down out of the truck and slump into the house. He follows them into the house past their mother and into their bedroom, off the kitchen. With them in their beds and asleep again as if it had never been broken, he crosses the kitchen to the open door and looks out toward the woods and the mill. "Sit down," she says to his back where he stands in the door. "You got time for breakfast."

She was still talking, but since we had heard the story so many times before, we had finished before her, at least I had, and I waited for her to finish, her voice still swirling in the dim light overhead, darting at remembered details in the dark of her history like the other night birds in the further dark above us. I was getting uncomfortable sitting, so I changed my position and looked out at the clutter of the town beyond the yard's edge. In these last months it had struck me as having the shape and order of so many leaves blown against a curb, like her, left over, living on in a love that had lasted from that time to this. It drew its only life from the railroad tracks that stitched its sides, and when the line was abandoned, it would be too. While her voice went on, I finished the rest of the story myself. The mill did not succeed, nor did Grampa's other plans. Eventually, his children and the other relatives fled to the cities and were swallowed up to eventually die in them. To me, the end of the story was Grampa's death in 1948, and the rest, my parents' and aunt's and uncle's deaths, in the years following, was *my* history. I was ready to go. As I saw her gliding for new territory, Grampa's attempt to make a go of a store in the early forties, I headed her off. "And then he had a hard time telling them, Gram," I said. You had to punctuate her stories or there'd be no end to them. "That was your way in those years. You loved and you got by. You brought us, all of your children, from then till now and you can be proud of that. Dear, work in the morning. You take care of yourself and we'll see you in a few days."

In the quiet of her having stopped talking, I was shouting at her as if she were deaf. In the silence after my own voice, she sat looking straight ahead. Then she said, "He couldn't tell them."

"That's right, Gram. He didn't tell them and it only shows what kind of people you were. You . . ."

"He couldn't tell them, and he kept them on until *none* of us could make a living out of the mill. When that failed, he tried the store. Then that . . . he could not shoot the horses," she said again. "And he could not let the Farrells go."

"Right, Gram," I said, but it was unnecessary. She was finally quiet.

In her final silence the night sounds floated back to us along with other, newer, sounds. From the house trailers to either side came the sounds of banging dishes, protesting children—the day's domestic squabbles being rekindled like evening fires. Somebody couldn't find the mate to their best sock, somebody absent, a father in a downtown bar, would get a cold supper. My wife's eyes said it was time to go and I agreed. As far as I was concerned, Grandma's story was over and it was time. It was any family's story—hard times and generations of troubles, but with love they had gotten through. She was near the end of her life, but it had been full and good. She didn't need me to tell her this. She didn't need us to confirm her story. She had told it again and we had listened and that was enough.

My wife and I rose from the porch steps to go. Grandma sat between us and did not look up. Her hands folded on themselves in her lap where she still stiffly sat on her wooden kitchen chair. From where we stood looking down at her, I saw her thinking *late* and *name:* name, that special felt quality that over the years takes on less of a sense of sound by which a family signs itself and more of a physical sense—a similarity in voices, gaits, postures, the shapes of mouths and eyes, cheekbones, chins, the lengths of body bones, the fit of clothes, all coming together as if all the faces were one face, all the bodies one body. . . . Against the pens behind us I saw the haunches of horses disappearing in the dark leaves, easy, out of time, then Grampa in his goodness leading the bay back out of the pens, its towel blinders still on, the rifle bolt thrown back.

Then my wife and I said goodbye. We said it at the same time and because we did, we almost didn't hear it. It came from somewhere in the off light, and in the confusion of the crickets and the frogs and the bickering in the trailers to either side we almost didn't hear it. From wherever, it came at us and held us where we were—tiny, piping, circling higher on itself like a killing bird. "Weak," she said quietly. "He was weak. All of this," her arm left her lap and described in the air what would have been a wide sweep before her that would take in the property, the town, her life, her children's, and ours, "could have been different." She looked up then and in her eyes was the look of someone who had for months been telling her story to people who could not or would not understand. "All different. All of it," she said. "Who do you know can't shoot a horse? Who do you know?"

As we walked to the car, she was still sitting on the porch. She was not yet ready to go back in and she would carry her own chair.

Later, while finding our way home over that road

that I had always thought I knew, it changed from moment to moment before me. *Grandma was old, the past was the past, the future was another matter.* But in that time of day's treacherous light, stretches of road I'd trusted to be straight became dangerous curves; curves insidiously straightened to become tediously endless. Around me the familiar seemed stricken, and the night lay ahead, waiting.

DARING

Our fifteenth summer, being too old to play cars and too young to drive them, we walked streets and woods and beaches, randy in our jeans, looking for girls, challenging each other as to whether we would know what to do if we found them. We were shy in our meanness, but too mean to hide our general boredom with summer vacation. Each of us hid our private cache of soft porn from drugstore shelves while in our hearts we preferred the sanctuary of brassiere sections in mail-order catalogs, where a modicum of cloth kept our blood from boiling while we envisioned the unholy things from a distance. Among ourselves we teased and cavilled, tripped up and slapped, caught at crotches and grabbed ass and generally shoved and pushed each other through the walls of stifling summer days. We broke streetlights, raided gardens, ducked chores, stole from our parents' purses, and got on their and our own nerves. None of us *sat* in houses; rather, we lolled with feet on walls. We rose high in the air to snag game-saving hits off doorway arches and left our fingerprints to show that we had been there. After each brilliant catch, phantom cheers echoing in our ears, we fell back to the carpeted outfield, cursing the weight of our own gravity. Through doors that always slammed after us, our shoulders hunched to clear the jambs, we flung ourselves into backyards, threw the tonnage of our weight around, came to standstill stops, and stymied ourselves with the question *what in the hell to do next.*

Our only salvation that summer came in the form of Aaron Gerndt, a goofy-looking kid our age who moved to town in mid-June. His father had lost a job somewhere in Minnesota and God had sent him, we thought, to our town to open up a small-engine repair shop at the crumbling end of our downtown street. He was God-sent, we cheered in our dark hearts, because he had brought Aaron with him. Aaron had not wanted to come, but like us, he was at the age of extremely limited choices.

Beneath the cruel stubble of his butch-cropped hair, cut by his father with clippers with guides, Aaron's ears were a comic relief in our heat-slugged three-act play. They stood stiffly out from his head and in a week earned him the name of Dumbo. Bunched in the middle of these thick wings were puzzled brows, a spread nose, and a loose, wandering mouth that sometimes tried to shape a response to our abuse but then pursed while his Adam's apple rode up to swallow down his pride. Like us, he was bored; unlike us, he was new in town and hard up for friends. We had someone where we wanted him.

In an effort to ingratiate, Aaron shared everything he owned. Plowing through the kitchen door into the backyard he would, at one stern look from any of us, divide his sandwich and share it. All candy of Aaron's was to be split four ways. Change found deep in the litter of chair or sofa cushions was community property. By the end of June, he was thoroughly instructed in the ways of our communism and like a true believer he gave dutifully. In return, we gave only the valued prize of our company.

One night while walking home from the movies in the aftermath of a two-gun double feature, Aaron revealed a quirk that gave him full membership in our fraternity. It was a tight, hot night that made breathing hard and predicted sticky, restless sleep on top of bed covers. After three hours of satisfying western violence where the body count was only barely exceeded by the number of shots fired, we walked home in distracted disconsolation. Now and then we gave each other hip-checks and fired at passing cars down the barrels of our pointer fingers. For a while we stopped and watched as Aaron and Jerry, the youngest in our group, fell out on the strip of grass between the sidewalk and the road and lunged at each other in a wrestling match. It was boring except when they rolled close to the curb, where car wheels slicked along less than a foot from their heads. We would have called out to them, but we didn't. Our wantonness was that keen and their danger too delicious. But in the end nobody got killed. Jerry rubbed at grass stains on his pants and merely mumbled, "Peckerhead," over and over, believing as we all did that summer that a well-placed epithet, if repeated long enough, could turn defeat to victory as surely as a spine-severing karate chop. Aaron limped along on a sprung groin muscle, his chafed, spiky head glowing like a taillight in the late evening summer sun. He mumbled a Scandinavian curse of some kind. We plodded home unsated. On the lowering edge of this night's darkness we could understand vampires.

As we angled down the most boring streets in town, those closest to our houses, we started to pass, then stopped in front of, old man Myron's house. His house was like him, squat, wide, sunk deep in its luxuriating lawns. Myron was famous in the neighborhood for his and his dog's mean spirits, a wife he treated worse than the dog, and lawns and a garden that he tended with the care a monk might give his soul. Last week, during one of our late-night raids on his sacred garden, he had caught Cliff and me by the hair and kicked our asses until we howled. Some of his kicks had landed between the legs in an area whose natural state was dull pain. In the growing darkness we stood on the street and in lowered voices cursed him to the flames at the center of the earth. At our side, ears cocked like a good dog ready to please, Aaron stood looking confused and quizzical. He hadn't been with us, and when Cliff and I explained, he merely said in a voice empty of all doubt or emotion, "Why don't you throw a rock through his window?" When we did not reply but rather stared off into the darkness as if we were hearing someone calling, he had his answer. "I thought so," he said.

"You thought what?" I said. He sounded like someone else. Facing him straight on, I said again, "You thought what?" But his moment had come and passed and he lapsed back into his standard stance—stomach out, shoulders round, his head like a vulture's sunk between them. Yet in his eyes there burned a small flame that, once lit, would not go out even in the gale of my questions. They were small fires, of the kind found buried deep in the floors of burned forests that weeks later flare up to level acres more. They were steady, and he warmed in their glow. "I will if you dare me," he said. We couldn't believe what we were hearing, but dare him we did, and then with the sound of the crash like an Easter hymn in our ears and a vision of shattered, shimmering glass leaping in shards in all directions, we pounded down alleys and behind garages through a thoroughfare of trash cans, fences, barbecue pits, and howling dogs until when we finally arrived at our destination, we didn't know where we were, only that we were blocks away from Myron. Sagging to the grass by the upturned belly of a stored boat, we lay there until our breath came back, then slowly eased down a driveway and headed home. That night as we lay stuck to our bed covers, our own fires burned lower, then somewhere toward morning snuffed out, and we slept the best sleep of the summer, waking way past noon, when the sun was heat-hazy and, like us, high.

None of us called him Dumbo again. That day, for the first time, we called for him at *his* house, the worst on our block. He came to the door, his face sleep-slack, his lips rubber, and wearing an expression on his face that even in its stupor seemed to say that he deserved a new respect. Later in his yard, while he sluffed into tennies and pulled on a T-shirt, we asked him if he had heard anything. He hadn't, but he didn't seem to care. Had we? We hadn't. Still later, as planned, we staggered our departure times by a half hour and one by one strolled down Myron's street to view the damage. We all saw, in the space of two hours, Myron sitting in a lawn chair with his dog at his side while two men cleaned out the remains of the old window and down through the afternoon fitted in and glazed a new one. At the drugstore, where we met in a back booth, we all agreed that Myron looked like the devil himself, and just as red. We were, for the moment, satisfied. Except me. Something that afternoon coiled slowly inside me and I heard its low rattle. I knew it then for what it was but put it out of mind. By day's end it had retreated back into the summer's torpor, like something slipped under the cool of a rock, and I slept soundly and deeply again. The next morning summer had a new, mixed meaning and I went out to meet it.

When you and all your closest friends are fourteen, months matter. I was the oldest, the closest to me being five months away. I had been in the world longer, I was believed to know more of the world's secrets, and to augment this I told terrific lies to cinch the position of leader. Being the leader of our small band that summer—that summer of limited friends, all male, and even more limited options—being the leader that summer was my one possession and I would not lose it. Of the lies I told to secure it there were many—some were banal but effective and prized highly for their impact, some were stock but could be counted on to command attention, and some were so stunning as to leave even me struck and wondering while staring at my bedroom ceiling in the light from a moon hung at the window. Without really knowing it, I had limited them to specific categories so that their subject matter would compel interest—cars, physical prowess, sex. To my group of slack-jawed disciples gathered at my feet behind someone's garage or draped over teeter-totters, say, in our town's small park, I wove images in the air over their heads that left them writhing like spiders on a hot plate. When I finished, the eyes in the heads of the lot of them would be out of focus, they could have tripped on their own tongues, and some of them, when I was at my best, would roll on the ground, their hands throttling their crotches, saying, "Shoot me, shoot me." Even Aaron, at whom I directed the wildest of my fabrications, sat looking up, enthralled.

But in the end it was all just talk. Eventually, we would get up from our places and look around for something to do. We knew in our hearts that we would wait for nightfall for whatever it was and that we would do it under cover of darkness. We raided more gardens, even Myron's, we cut string fences around new grass, in the lowering hours of early dark we broke streetlights and streaked for cover. But it was all done in the dark and later, in bed, and then even later, in the morning, it did not satisfy. Nobody had seen us, nobody had chased us—our stealth in the dark had been so successful that there had never been any danger. We had only slept soundly the night of Aaron's dare.

June was gone and July lazed in—flat, heat-laden, signing our summer away. In my own case, our household was too busy to care. My mother and father were gone to work by the time I got up and walked through a shower and breakfast and out the door into brilliant mornings where I spun on my hook like the wind chimes on our porch. Not wanting to be the first at anyone's door, I waited. Then, if no one showed up, I went looking.

Some mornings I awoke to discover that they had gone off to do things without me. I sulked through the neighborhood alone, thrashing my thoughts and squaring my shoulders. On these days it seemed as if everyone in the world had something to do and someplace they had to be. And someone to be with. I studied women talking in yards and men side by side on construction sites. Downtown, deep in the day's commerce, people spoke and smiled in stores and offices. On the streets they poked one another, shook hands, and slapped backs. Their talk was purposeful, animated, and always it was important that they be right where they were, in their place, at this time. Without them exactly there, businesses would halt, new buildings would cease to rise, families would perish from neglect. Unnoticed and unnecessary, I moved invisibly among them, envying even the lowest their menial tasks.

On some of those days, I later found out, they had gone to Aaron's house without me. His house was different. Once when Jerry asked him where his mother was, Aaron only said, "Gone." He didn't say any more. He just sucked his lower lip, and when he let it out, he talked about something else.

Their clothes lay in heaps where they had dropped them. His father's were gray and black and smelled of oil. In the living room, potato-chip bags and beer bottles stood up from the floor and balanced on the arms of chairs. At times the rim of a plate or dish stuck out from under a couch or TV stand. Beds were not made. On the kitchen table bottles of ketchup remained permanently, with mustard, salt and pepper, peanut butter and jelly jars, crusted silverware, and diminishing slabs of butter melting in saucers. Slices of bread dominoed out of wrappers and stiffened. There was no sign of a woman's hand anywhere in all the rooms. No curtains hung at the windows, just yellowed shades drawn down tight to the sills. I liked going there and I knew I wouldn't want to live there.

In his house, with his father not home, Aaron strutted and flaunted his man's life-style. He swore more than usual and swaggered through the rooms puffing himself up to more clearly show us his perfect freedom. He called his father by his first name and spoke of their shared adventures and plans. They were buddies, equals. One time he even sipped from a warm half-bottle of beer and relit a cigarette butt from an ashtray. We were Tom Sawyers to his Huck Finn, but his Pap was a good guy.

On the days that followed the ones when I was not invited to Aaron's house, I did not mention the fact when we met again. Instead, I let it be known that I had had things to do.

Afternoons were the longest. By then the sun was high, the heat hard, and whatever damp promise morning had held had dried. We swam, we scuffed through stores fingering but not buying, we griped, talked dirty, and moped. We looked at car speedometers through windows to see how fast they could go. We straddled untended motorcycles on their kickstands and rubbed their leather and steel between our legs. We gaped at girls indiscriminately everywhere, in stores, on the streets, in windows, and on beaches. We stared, teased, insulted, and harassed, but we did not touch. We shouted what we thought were good pick-up lines learned from watching older boys in cars who cruised movie theaters and beaches, their elbows hooked to steering wheels, their eyes slitted. "Hey, baby, you hot?" "Wanna see what I got for you?" "Ya wanna? Ya wanna?" But none of them did. Rather, they laughed at us as they twitched away with their precious cargo as if they could see through our clothes and spy out our tiny swellings for what they were. And in our secret hearts we were glad that they didn't want to, though we admitted this to no one, especially each other. Only later in our celibate cells did we barely and then uncertainly admit it to ourselves.

Aaron dared. One afternoon when we were downtown, we watched two cops on a coffee break through a diner window. Someone said that the air should be let out of their cruiser's tires which was parked out front. For a moment the prospect of its happening was out of the question and then, as if of one mind, we turned to Aaron. Did he dare? He did, and in broad daylight on our busiest street he crawled from wheel to wheel. He twisted valve caps and pressed stems until the car sank unceremoniously with its antennae and pursuit lights and insignia to the ground. When he was finished, he rose up to walk to where we lurked in an alley. When we took off running, we could hear his calm voice behind us saying, "What's the hurry?" Blocks later, when he caught up to us in Cliff's backyard, he pushed through sheets on a clothesline and said nonchalantly, "You guys see a ghost or something?"

In the days that followed, Aaron dared to do even more. With his shoulders thrown back and his chin out, nothing short of human possibility daunted him. When he was presented with a challenge, you could have struck a match on his eye. As our own Jolly Roger he flew our principal's boxer shorts from the school flagpole. In early August, on Jerry's back porch, he rose to a dare to steal a car and while we sat in disbelief he disappeared into the night and within an hour returned to rumble quietly up the alley in a Ford. We all climbed into it and rode around until the fuel gauge read *E,* and then abandoned it by a gas station on the edge of town.

Two or three afternoons a week Aaron had to work in his father's shop. I went there once to see him about our plans for the night. His father's place of business was an old storefront huddled between a hotel whose clientele had always been suspect and a seedy corner gas station where loiterers kept cans of beer in the pop cooler and drank them openly in the doorway. In my lifetime Aaron's father's shop had been a restaurant, a furniture-stripping concern, a pizza joint, and the last, which had folded the year before, a discount retread-tire outlet. Inside, working on a small motor, Aaron's father was bent over a cluttered workbench strewn with beer bottles. A cigarette sent up a stream of smoke into his eye. Aaron was further down the wall, washing parts in a trough and placing them on a table to dry. The air in the room was leaden, heavy with the burnt-oil smell of failed machinery. On the blackened floor, lawn mowers and snowblowers and outboard engines leaned against each other in corners, their covers off, cables and cords sprung from them like clock springs. Aaron waved to me when I came in but turned back to his work when his father looked up and saw me. His father's look wasn't pleasant and didn't mean to make me feel welcome. "If you've come for Aaron," he said, "he's got work to do today. You might as well head back on out."

"I just wanted to talk to him for a minute," I said.

"He ain't got no time for talking. Say what you got to say and then find your way out." After a hard look at me, he turned to Aaron. "You're gettin' your hair cut the first time I get a minute to myself. You hear me?"

"Yes, Pa," Aaron said.

"You watch your tone, boy, if you wanta keep takin' your meals sittin' down." Turning back to me, he said, "He ain't got no time to talk, boy. You better be takin' out for home." When I was outside again, I could hear Aaron's father shouting "good-for-nothing friends" and "lazy" followed by a stream of cursing until I turned and walked up the street.

The following days grew heavier with the coming of school. Class schedules appeared in our mailboxes. Stores downtown brandished BACK TO SCHOOL ads in their windows. Summer was closing down. During these days, Aaron ascended. He had grown these last months, as had his hair. Through a biological spurt he was nearly as tall as I was, and his father's haircut had grown out from its stippled mat to soft waves that flowed over and shrank his ears. His face, too, had lengthened. Only his mouth, with its tendency to slacken, its quick readiness to go either way, belied anything he had gained in the way of absolute assurance. When he looked me almost eye to eye toward the end of summer, in what I thought was his challenge for the leader of our band, his eyes would lock on mine for a moment and then duck and quit. Since that afternoon in his father's shop, we both knew that I had seen into the deepest intimacy of his life. It was our secret that we did not discuss. He, in turn, saw through me and now suspected my stories for what they were. We were bound to each other in silence.

With two weeks to go until September, we rushed to fill fourteen days with everything we could to shore us up for school's long winter. In the fall, we would all be high school freshmen and we knew in advance what our social stations would be. We would be the lowest on the totem pole, the butt of jokes, the victims of initiations by the upperclassmen. We had heard of "swirlies" in the school bathrooms, harassment by the "hall monsters," and locker-room rituals that we would have to endure as rites of passage. We discussed these things only once, then pushed them down into the deepest part of that summer and never mentioned them again. We were drawn during those final days to the beach, to the sun and sand and water, which seemed now to promise to preserve us through the coming cold, dark seasons. We got up earlier during those mornings in order to get as much as the days had to give. The beaches swelled and their special gift was throngs of girls as naked as the law would allow. They preened and primped and showed to best advantage what was theirs as they tricked by us on the rolling sands, then stretched, dove, and swam. In a long mural of skin, they untied and retied straps, poked at wayward flesh, and raised and lowered bits of cloth to the sun.

We arrived early and stayed late, until the setting sun and evening breeze spread chills over the sand and one by one the girls gathered up blankets and clothes until the beach was deserted. Then, when they were gone, we would get up too and head for home, each time less talkative than the last. The next day we were back by noon.

Labor Day was the last official day for the beaches to be open. They would close for the season at that day's end. The holiday brought a large crowd, this time whole families with picnic baskets, to swell the entire woodsy area with music and barbecue smoke and games of all kinds. Our families, except Aaron's, were there somewhere, but we tended to avoid them and hung out this last time together. We felt an air of urgency among us, an awareness that this was our last time to get what only summer could give.

We took up our positions on the grass behind the beach and for a while just surveyed the sand and water, both packed with more people than had ever been there at one time all summer. Mothers and babies waded while old men shuffled in the lace looped along the water's edge. The raft was so crowded that the people on it seemed to be standing on water. And for the last time, the girls were everywhere. We watched them until we needed cooling off and then dove in and swam for the raft.

High above what must have appeared to her as a motley crew, *she* sat in her white pith helmet and whitened nose and white bathing suit, the lifeguard, on her white lifeguard stand. Summer's high priestess in a Jantzen, she surveyed the goings-on, and with her whistle and megaphone she stopped games of tag, running on the beach, cannonballing, roughhousing on the raft, and generally any behavior she didn't care for. Her attitude was imperious and her rule over the beach as absolute as she was unreachable on her high perch. At one time during the afternoon, she pointed at the four of us and whistled us out of the water. Through her megaphone she talked down to us about the "rules of the raft" and how they left no room for pushing people over the side. Even friends. With an arbitrariness befitting her position, she thought for a moment and then said that we were to stay out of the water for a half-hour. With a sideways glance at her watch, she turned away from us and, dismissed, we walked, chastised, back to our places on the grass.

Her megaphone had made our sentence public, so in addition to our exile, we suffered as well the eyes of gawkers as they pointed us out to each other. A group of girls directly in front of us laughed and then turned their backs. *Her* back sat high above us, and from the ground we aimed remarks that would fall just short of reaching her.

Beneath her stand, in cardboard boxes was the beach litter stashed there by a morning grounds crew. Cellophane and paper and plastic flowed over their tops. While we stared at her royal back, someone said that we should set fire to the boxes. "Burn the bitch down," Cliff said.

"Give her a hot seat," Jerry piped in.

None of them looked to me. Instead, they turned to Aaron. His eyes swept the beach and the hundreds of people who would be witnesses. This would be the most daring yet, and the sheer courage of it stunned us into a long silence. Overhead, a cloud covered the sun in a slow passing and we sat in its chill. In the minutes before the cloud's lining lightened and the sun came out again, I stared at her and him as we waited for his response. I knew he would have to do it if he was dared, and the danger and the beauty of it grew until finally I turned to him. "Go ahead, Aaron," I said. "I dare you."

"Why don't you?" he said, and the corner of his mouth worked a little.

"Because you're the daredevil," I said. "Burn her down, if you dare. That's your thing, you know." His eyes held mine, and though no tears came, they asked *why* in a way that I understood. This time I dropped my eyes.

She escaped with only a singed pride and the scorched stand was doused with buckets brought up from the lake. By this time Aaron was long gone. When the police arrived, they followed witnesses' descriptions and accounts and began their search down the wooded lakeshore. A few hours later they caught him and brought him back to the beach for identification. Then they loaded him into the back of their cruiser. He sat tight to the window, and as they drove him away, his last look was for me.

The juvenile court ruled that his act was more than a childish prank and that he needed rehabilitation. In a week he was sent away to a reform school. A month later his father's business failed and he too packed up and moved on.

That fall I threw myself into my schoolwork and burned up my spare time in extracurricular activities. I survived what the upperclassmen thought were trying tests and I wondered why they had held such fear for me. The girls were there, but as fall grew heavier so did their clothing, and that fire burned a little lower. A few times Cliff and Jerry and I met after school and walked home together, but as the colder months set in, we drifted apart. When I walked past Aaron's house, I often thought of wherever they had taken him, this time to a place where his courage could get him into trouble that could unutterably alter his life. To me the windows in his house could have been those in the police cruiser, and as I was drawn to look into them, I saw again his last look for me. Eventually, I began taking another way home.

T.E. DIBBLE

STATIONS

When Al Parish's youngest son accidentally shot the Watt boy down in the Alder swamp, where the swamp breaks up and leaks into the lake through the stumps and skags and the geese hold up in their fall flight, when he did that, accidentally blew out the boy's stomach while he was clearing the breech of his new pump twelve-gauge that Al had bought for him the day before, Al did right by the Watt boy, what we would have expected of him. He took the boy to the hospital at the county seat in the back of his panel truck, and once they were there, he hired a private nurse to be with him until he was well. From what we heard, it was touch-and-go for some weeks, what with that load of three-shot having blown a hole the size of a baseball in his middle. He was in the hospital for four months, and when he got out he wasn't much good for the kind of work he had been brought up to. His father and brothers were all loggers, and there was no way that he could log. He healed, but anything that involved lifting or bullwork was out of the question. So, Al sold him the little gas station next to his store on our main street. Gave it to him, some said. We never heard the price, but since the Watts never had any money to speak of, we knew it couldn't have been much. The Watts' house always had about it in its low, dark rooms a mustard-yellow cast and the constant odor of a hot stove and meat. The house itself was a small frame one, black on the outside, tar paper. Inside were four rooms of equal size with low ceilings, each room punished with cast-off furniture (some of it out of the Parish house, we had heard), homemade beds of sorts, guns, traps, saws, fishing poles, and people. There had been nine people in Jack Watt's family. The smokiness in the rooms, a density that hung like ground fog, came from a large pot on a wood-burning range where wildlife of all kinds and in all seasons was cooking, the idea being to boil it off the bone until you could eat it, which you did in that house even if you had to do it standing up.

This is a small town with about one, and only one, of everything—one bar, one bait shop, one boat rental, one hotel, one barbershop, and one gas station. The only things that there are two of are the churches, a Catholic and a Protestant, and stores. Parish owned one of the stores, and Gunnard, the other. Whether it was a law that Parish and Gunnard signed their names to or shook hands on or maybe just a notion they lived by for so long that it congealed into law, nobody really knows. As it was, neither of them stocked what the other carried in his store and for years they drove the thirty miles to the county seat together to get their supplies, taking their turns in Parish's panel truck or Gunnard's pickup. We all knew this and so we never went to their stores expecting to find what the other carried.

The gas station was about fifty feet from Parish's store, a small cement block building with, inside, a counter stocked with some automotive accessories and random fishing lures and odds and ends. On the wall behind was a rack for cigarettes and a shelf for candy. Outside, by a corner of the building, was a hand-cranked drum of kerosene for the camps around the lake and out front was a single gas pump. It was the only gas pump in town. The town's size being what it was, we didn't need more than one. Half the time we'd pump our own and then walk over to pay Al what we owed him. He never questioned the amount.

So, Al sold him the station. Selling it must have triggered something in him because within a month he had sold everything else he owned as well. The first thing was the store, that to Gunnard, and then his lake properties, and then what timber holdings he had up on the grade. Within a month he had sold it all and by May he was gone, gone to Florida, he said, to get the sun that you'd never see in northern Michigan if you lived to be a hundred.

Then Daryl, the Watt boy, owned the station. When we'd pull in we'd try to pump our own as we had in the past, but he wouldn't hear of it. He'd run out of the station and put the hose in the tank and then he'd come up front and check under the hood, and when he was satisfied that everything was all right, he'd close it down and start scrubbing on the windshield and squeegeeing it down. We'd see him up through our windshields, happy and intense, his face, moonlike, leaning over to look down into the car to see if what he did pleased. A few times during the first weeks the puddles of gas behind the car spoke to his need to time his services to his enthusiasm, but he was a good boy and a hard worker. The station and he were good for each other.

And Gunnard owned both of the stores. At first we didn't see any changes. His wife stayed on to run the old store and he moved into Parish's. Each week he'd drive in his pickup to the county seat like always, but then, in a month or so, it was in a newer, bigger van that he bought on one of his trips so that he could haul enough for both stores in fewer trips. The prices in both stores went up slightly, but we understood that, what with his increased overhead and nobody to share traveling expenses with.

And so things went on pretty much as they had in the past. It was spring then and the tourists came back and the town's pace picked up. The fishing on the lake was good, and because it was, the hotel was almost always full. Dick Fulton could hardly keep his bait bins and tanks full, and he kept half the young town boys in work digging worms by day or picking crawlers off lawns by night or seining minnows with his kids out in the lake shallows. All of this went to keep the hotel guests sitting hunched over his brother Ted's outboards as they pointed his boats out toward the walleye and bass and perch beds. And Daryl was kept busy pumping gas into Ted's drums that he'd bring to the station in the back of his pickup. That plus his regular business got Daryl off to a nice start, and we were glad for that because we all knew that in the winter, business would be slow.

Gunnard was busy, too. He had always been a hard worker, and now that he owned both stores, he had to work that much harder. He didn't have the time to talk much like before, but that was understandable. He didn't only run the stores, he improved them and in front of his new store (he still called it Parish's: he didn't like the tourists to know that he owned both) he spread crushed white rock and added flower boxes full of geraniums to the front of the building. He did the work himself and that, in addition to putting a new roof on the old store and running them both, kept him busy. There was some talk that he could have farmed out the work to the Stanton brothers, who had always done Parish's work, but that died out when they got work on some construction project down at the county seat.

And then before we knew it, there was yellow in the trees. Spring had come up to its full green and the green stayed and the weather warmed and so did we. Then the green yellowed and the tourists left and we were left to ourselves. There was the fall to come, that and the hunting and the hunters' suppers at both the churches. But then it would be winter. Winter meant that it would be dark at five o'clock.

When we heard about Daryl's upcoming marriage, we were not surprised. He and Dick Fulton's girl had been going together for two years at the time when the Parish boy had shot him. For the last few months, being small-boned and fragile as she was, Dick's girl had displayed her pregnancy around town in a way reminiscent for some of us of the starving, wide-eyed native waifs in *National Geographic* who proudly carry their distended bellies for the photographers as if their size were a badge of health. She showed up on Daryl's arm pert like a puffer pigeon at local ball games and at the lake park on Sundays as if being sixteen and pregnant and unmarried were as natural as what they had done to get that way.

It was held in the Protestant church on a Saturday in early October and the whole town turned out for it. Daryl's bride, like him, had about her face that surprised look of the undernourished, something childlike and hopefully expectant: large-eyed, undersized, she walked up the aisle in her married sister's altered wedding gown in tentative steps, as if at any minute the gown would change into jeans and a shirt and she would be hip deep in the lake shallows throwing seining nets before her with her brothers on either side, instead of Daryl and her father marching her up a church aisle to her own wedding. After the wedding we all went down to the church basement to get our lunches and brought them out to the side lawn to eat. The weather was soft, with small breezes and the smell of leaves in it. Everyone milled around until Daryl and his new bride left in her father's car for a two-day honeymoon, and then most of us went down to the bar and finished the party there.

Our final community event for the season was the hunters' supper hosted by both the churches for the out-of-town hunters who were hunting the deer in our area. The profits usually provided enough money to heat the churches during the winter, so everybody did their best to make it a success. The men did the cooking in the churches' basements, and the women and children waited on tables out front. It was during this time that Gunnard first showed signs of a change. In the past, his and Parish's contribution to the event was usually a few cases each of breads and rolls and tins of coffee. We had come to expect it over the years and so we were surprised when this year he told the women that he couldn't afford it and instead offered to give it to them at cost. His explanation for the change was his high overhead which, he was sure, he said, they would understand. They didn't, but they told him that they did. What else could they do, they asked the rest of us, what with the supper being the next day? Anyway, cost was better than full price. We had to agree to that, but still it was a change from the way things used to be.

This winter our outings were brightened with visits to Daryl's gas station. Framed in the building's single front window banked with snow up to its lower sill, he and his young wife sat in Daryl's tiny office in their warmest clothes as close to the space heater as possible. Even as they bulked in their winter clothing, they appeared childlike still. As one of us pulled up to the pump outside, they would race each other out the door, pushing and shoving and catching each other up like cub bears to see who would be first to wait on us. For all of that, Daryl was always careful and deferred to her no matter who won the race and let her pump the gas while he went about his business under the hood and saw to our windows and tires.

Some days Daryl wouldn't be there, as he would be up in the woods with his father and brothers helping them with their logging operation. He couldn't do much other than drive the truck, what with his stomach being as it was, but he did what he could to help. That's how we found out about Parish's timber holdings. Gunnard had bought them. He had bought them and had sold the timber rights to the mill the Watt family was logging for. Jack Watt told us that Gunnard had bought all of Parish's four hundred acres and that the pine and maple were to come down because Gunnard needed the money for improvements in the stores. Jack said that he had last seen Gunnard in the snow up on a ridge of birch shouting about something and waving his hands in the timber cruiser's face and that then Gunnard had disappeared over the ridge and the cruiser had headed back down to where they were cutting in the pine stand. Jack said that the cruiser had been miserable to work around and that he and his boys had stayed out of his way and had cut ahead of him as much as they could all day. The next day, Jack said, the cruiser sent him and his boys up on the ridge to cut the birch that Gunnard said were to come down. The cruiser told Jack that the birch were too young, that they hadn't gotten their growth yet, but to cut them anyway because Gunnard said so and who was he to say against an owner; he was only a timber cruiser with thirty years in the trade.

It wasn't too long after that that we heard there was some trouble between Gunnard and his wife. She was a short, round woman whom for years we had seen mostly from the waist up as she stood behind the counter in their first store and smiled and called out to us as we came in. Over the years, she had aged gracefully and it was impossible for us to think of the store without the real pleasure of her being in it. She knew whatever there was to know about what was good in the town and so she gave us that while she gave us our groceries in a bag. She was another part of what we had always thought of as Gunnard's good luck: he had married well. When she first started to change, the changes were slight. She no longer smiled at us as we came into the store; at times she would be sitting down behind the counter with only her head showing, listening to the radio, acting as if the bell over the door were sounding in some other county and it wasn't her place to answer it. Other times, after we'd entered the store she'd disappear into the back room and come out only when she figured we were ready to pay for our purchases. When we made them, she'd merely nod to our comments about someone's new baby or new job or new car. Nobody's small successes interested her. Large successes drew her eyes down and made ours turn away. This lasted and grew throughout the winter until finally (a difference we had come to rely on without knowing it) there was not much difference between the gray cold outside the store and that inside. The meanness grew in her and diminished her until finally it was simply a presence, like bad air in a closed room. And so we got out as quickly as we could, leaving her to bear with the store and herself. And then in late winter she left.

The talk was that she couldn't stand working all the hours in the store and had told Gunnard so, but that he didn't think he could afford to take on help at the time. He had told her, the talk went, that in the spring, when the tourists were back and the business was up again, at that time they would look into the possibility of hiring someone to spare her. But it wasn't enough, she had said, and for no good reason that we could discover. She would go to live with her sister for a while in Illinois to think it over. Someone who saw her the day she left, sitting next to Gunnard in his van while he went to the county seat to get his supplies and to drop her off at the airport, said it looked to him like she had done all the thinking she was going to do about it and that it appeared that Gunnard would before long be looking for more than just someone to work in his store.

We felt sorry for Gunnard then. He hadn't done anything any man wouldn't do. He was trying to get by and, beyond that, to make something of himself. He had become in a way a sort of model for some of the younger people in the town who were just starting out. He was hard-working, he didn't ask anyone to work any harder than he did himself, and his improvements to the stores were plain for anyone to see. Then, too, for a man to have his wife leave him in a town our size, where everyone knows everyone's business, for everyone to know his embarrassment and, worse yet, his loneliness—all of this, we felt, must have added to his burden of dealing with her absence. When we talked about it, we used the word *absence* for the first few months and then, because of the length of time she had been gone and the further talk we had heard, *absence* was at some point changed to *loss* and we were reconciled to it whether he was or not.

In the meantime Gunnard had hired someone, Mrs. Stone, a widow, to work in the other store. Having to pay a separate salary cut into his profits, but he stayed on in Parish's, and now that it was spring again and the tourists were coming back to rent lake cabins or hotel rooms or to repair the winter damages to their own cabins, his hardware and sporting-goods sales were up again. The warmer weather revived him as it did all of us and projects brought him outdoors again, so that gradually the winter pallor left his face and he appeared more his old self again. In May someone even said that they had seen him and Mrs. Stone driving out of town in the evening, possibly to go to a movie or a dinner down at the county seat. We could only guess as to whether this was true, but we hoped it was. Mrs. Gunnard had the papers in the works for a divorce.

He had had enough bad luck and nobody wished him any worse. What had gone on between him and Mrs. Gunnard was nobody's business, we felt, because who is to say what should be somebody's ways as long as they are hard-working and their ways don't intrude on anybody or bring them harm? Gunnard's ways were no different from Parish's or those of the men before them, who had built the town and owned things in it, things like stores and mills and property, things that made a difference because the men who owned them did. It was no sin to be a success if it came from hard work with maybe a little luck thrown in. As far as Mrs. Gunnard, she could have helped him by trying to understand, by giving him a little more time. Since she had chosen not to, *instead* had simply chosen to *leave,* our sympathies were with him, not her.

Because we knew that Gunnard was not much of a drinker, we were surprised when he came into the bar on a Saturday afternoon and by appearances had been drinking before he got there. His face was flushed as he came through the door and his speech thick as he came up to the bar, where a half-dozen of us were talking to Les behind the bar. He stood up to the bar and waved his hand over our drinks to signal a round of drinks to Les. He was very excited, more so than we had seen him be in a long time, so we turned to him to see what was the cause. Some of us thought his news would have been about Mrs. Stone. We had heard about a possible marriage.

"If you need those drinks as much as I need mine," he said, "you won't leave them sitting on the bar." He raised his glass in a shaky toast to something in the air. We halfheartedly toasted with him and waited for him to tell us.

"Sink or swim," he said.

"What do you mean?" someone said.

"Just that. This time all or nothing. I put up both stores and my house to buy Parish's cabins from that outfit in Chicago."

"The rentals on the lake?" Lloyd asked.

"All of 'em. All nine of 'em," Gunnard said, and put his glass on the bar for a refill.

"What about the Chicago outfit?"

"They found 'em too hard to look after this far north, so they put 'em on the block. I bought them and the land. A half-mile of lake frontage. The stores and the house are up as collateral."

"All of it?"

"All of it. If I make it, make it pay, I'm in. If I don't. . . ."

"How long do you have," I asked.

"Not long enough," he said, and drained his glass. "But we do these things, don't we." He looked at us with a stunned look, his eyes a little out of focus. But then he brightened and said, "What the hell?" and talked to us about the lake level and how the bass were doing.

He was a little distracted for the rest of the afternoon and he left us standing at the bar and went to the jukebox. He put in enough money for a half-dozen songs and then went to the pool table, where he racked up the balls for rotation and played both sides for a while. Then he put more money in the jukebox and went and sat in a booth. Les brought him drinks for another hour or so and then he left the bar. When he left, we knew that because of what he had done his life from now on would be altered. Most people simply go along in life becoming more like themselves, only older, but Gunnard's life had taken a turn that would change him in some way, a pivotal moment of the kind that sharpens and traces the outlines of some men so that they are seen clearly. The air in the bar for the rest of the afternoon was agitated.

So then he had both the stores, some timber property, and all of Parish's rental units. This threw him into pretty stiff competition with the hotel, but it only seemed fair and we watched him go after it. He hired the Stanton brothers this time to do the needed repairs to the lake cabins and within a month he had six of the nine rented for the season. The other three he advertised in the *Journal,* the county-seat paper, and at least one downstate paper. Nobody in our town had ever advertised anything. People either found their products and bought them or they didn't. Gunnard's ads ran:

> CABINS FOR RENT
> LIFE IN THE NORTH
> THE BEST OF FISHING AND HUNTING
> CALL M. GUNNARD
> LONG LAKE, MICHIGAN

and then his phone number. He filled two more cabins with walleye fishermen from Milwaukee. They had never heard of Long Lake, Michigan.

August came again and, with it, still, hot days heavy with the smell of the lake and grass and pine. Daryl's baby was already about four months old then and his wife couldn't help him in the gas station as much as she had before. She had her hands full with the baby and spent most of her time at home. Daryl worked from early morning until dark, and that and being a young father showed. His face darkened from hours spent working under cars and his thin shoulders sagged slightly under the slack of his coveralls. The only thing that showed of his handicap of his having been shot was the care he gave to his midsection when lifting anything or, say, working over his head removing oil filters or tail pipes. Shallow lines of strain, the marks of a man bearing up under the weight of responsibility, were beginning to lightly score the boyishness of his face.

Next to his gas station, Gunnard's store bustled with business. Lately it had become more than just a store. Now it was the center of all of his businesses and projects. His office in the back of the store had become the hub of his operations and it was there that he dealt with produce and meat distributors, salesmen and dealer representatives, realtors and renters come to pay their bills or just talk. The office had become so busy that one day we saw the Stanton brothers cutting a door through the outside wall and building a set of steps so that visitors to the office wouldn't have to file through the store aisles and disturb the shoppers.

Gunnard, we knew, had made it. The day that he had come into the bar and announced his decision now seemed a time out of the distant past, and everything that we had imagined that could possibly have happened as a result now seemed remote and no longer had the cutting edge of probability about it. He had not lost everything. The lost look about his eyes that day when he had said, "We do these things, don't we," the lost look that had singled him out from all of us who did not do "those things" was gone now and we knew it had not only been temporary but more, an illusion, and it was ours. His gaze had always been steady and his vision clear. If the decision had weakened him temporarily he was stronger now, perhaps because of it. It was as apparent as the difference between his new car and those we drove, as his girlfriend's new clothes and those we could afford to buy for our wives.

With his gains in property and business came the addition of new friends for Gunnard. He joined some of the men's social and business clubs down at the county seat, and so a couple of times a week he would drive there to have lunch with them. When he spoke to us, he often mentioned names we had only read in the paper for one reason or another—doctors, lawyers, a bank president once. Then, too, his new friends came to visit him and he would throw parties for them at one of his lake cabins, where they would play cards for big money, we heard, the lights in the cabin burning until sunrise sometimes. One time a group came up to one of his parties in a seaplane and taxied right across the front of the lake park and Ted Fulton's boat dock on its way to Gunnard's cabin. We men didn't say anything about any of this. There was nothing that could be put into so many words. It was just something we knew, in a way a man knows his own illness but doesn't tell his doctor, telling himself instead that if the doctor doesn't find it, then he doesn't have it.

What happened next did so in such a hurry as to take us all by surprise. To save money and to consolidate his operations, Gunnard decided to close the old store and have a large addition built onto the main one. Before we knew it, a contracting firm was in town and in a matter of weeks a large metal-sheeted addition stood attached to the store and nearly doubled its size. Gunnard hired extra people to stock the new addition, and after a couple of days and nights, when lights burned late at night and into the early-morning hours, the job was finished. A sign in the window announced a grand opening with prizes and games in a matter of a few days. Someone in the window in the bar across the street from where we watched the late-night activity said that Gunnard knew where to put his prizes and games. Someone else said that if *he* wanted a prize of some kind, he would buy his own. He didn't need Gunnard to buy it for him. A third person in the crowd said that he could imagine the prizes—overpriced pieces of junk that Gunnard had not been able to sell in either of his stores. If one of them had *his* name on it, Gunnard could keep it, *thank you,* and *Mr. G.* needn't expect him to show up, *hat in hand,* at his door to claim it. And so it went. How long had Gunnard been gouging us with his high prices and inferior goods? How many stories had we heard about stale bread, sour milk, rotten produce, and damaged cans that if not watched could kill a man's family in the space of a single meal? How long could a person in good conscience continue to do business with a man who so overworked his wife as to drive her from her home, for that matter to another state, while he carried on with another woman?

When two days later we heard of something strange having gone on during the last night that the stock was being moved to the new store, of clothing and canned goods and cases of the new, lightweight fishing rods that somehow, mysteriously, did not complete the trip in the back of the truck from the one store to the other, *vanished into thin air,* the report went—when we heard of it, we said that it was a crime but that crime was up all over the country. All a person had to do was open any newspaper and look on any page. As for its being bad luck for Gunnard, all he had to do was to look a few feet from his office to see bad luck, see Daryl there from dawn to dusk, working under cars and pumping gas and doing all of this with a bad stomach to boot. That, we thought, should be enough for Gunnard or any man to teach him about responsibility and bad luck and the hard work it takes to balance the both of them.

Gunnard survived his losses (added their cost to the prices of our purchases, some said) and thrived in spite of his setback. Perhaps it was his minor losses or, more likely, his greed, but we were all unprepared for what he did next. His name had grown in the area to have the prominence by way of repetition of, say, the post office. He was a fixture in our days—we would tell our wives or they would tell us as they left the house with errand lists in their hands, "I'm going to check the mail and then to Gunnard's and then I'll be home." It was on any one of our days like this that we heard from Daryl that Gunnard had approached him about buying his station. Daryl had refused, saying that without it (and lacking a certified talent to trade on) he wouldn't be able to find much in the way of work that he could do. Gunnard, he said, pressed the matter for a few days, but then gave up when Daryl couldn't be persuaded.

In middle September, when the machines showed up, touches of winter, though the days were warm, were already in the air. Nights while standing on his porch a man could feel the sharp air out of the northwest and know it for the truth. Winter was coming and our warm days were merely pleasant lies to be enjoyed for as long as they might last. The day the machines arrived, a bulldozer and a crane on lowboys, to dig the hole and lower the gasoline storage tanks into the ground in front of Gunnard's store, the weather was especially warm and we were out in it. By noon our main street was filled with the roaring of the machines and the shouts of men as they pushed up tons of Gunnard's rock driveway to prepare a bed for the tanks. By nightfall the tanks were in the ground and the hole filled again, leaving only a raw surface like that of a freshly dug grave. The following day, another crew appeared to set up Gunnard's two new gas tanks and to erect his dealer's sign. His prices, we soon learned, were four cents less a gallon than Daryl's.

In the days that followed, we talked less about Gunnard's affairs than we had since Parish's boy had shot Daryl and Gunnard had bought out Parish's holdings. There was nothing to talk about. What he had done and what we had to do was clear. When we met, at the bar or at Daryl's or at the hunters' supper, we understood, without putting it into so many words, that winter coming on or not, he had crossed a line, a line, that whether he fully understood it or not, was a line. Whether he understood it, or his fiancée, or his doctor and lawyer friends and those with their own seaplanes, the line was a law. As it was, we all began to drive the thirty miles to the county seat for our groceries. At first the women said that it was too inconvenient to shop the one time for an entire week, but when we explained it, why it had to be done, they did it. For a month, on Saturdays when we would drive by we would see Gunnard standing in his store window looking out at the street, the lost look again in his eyes that had held us that day in the bar, the look lost but knowing. But that was all right. He had gone too far and this had to be done. We'd drive on and when we returned to town hours later, our week's shopping done, his lights in the store would be out and we went on home to bed. No local car pulled up to his gas pumps.

During that time, Gunnard took to coming to the bar regularly but stayed to himself. His routine was to come in and give a high sign to Les and then go to a back booth, where Les brought him his drinks. After drinking for an hour or so, he'd get up and put money in the pool table and play rotation by himself. He drank heavily while he played, then in an hour or so he'd leave. His habit as he left was to come up to the end of the bar and have a last shot of whiskey while Les cleared his tab at the till. His looks at us down the long bar were telling, but other than someone nodding a hello, nothing was said. At a point agreed upon without discussion, a point at which we all stared as if at a phantom, he along with us would head for home, something having gone out of the pleasure of our afternoon drinking and card playing.

Within weeks, Mrs. Stone was gone from town and we heard about Gunnard's money problems with his ex-wife and some money owed to the Stanton brothers for their work on his holdings. Later they said that Gunnard had had to let some payments lapse on the lake cabins and that even with his bank president friend working on his side there was nothing that could be done and the bank took them from him. Whatever had possessed him to go after the gas business too we couldn't tell, but he did and now it was over. The same day the gas company came to take down its sign, a CLOSED sign appeared in his store window.

As for us men, mostly that fall we stayed each to himself. A few of us, because it was the season, put together a partridge hunt up on Parish's grade, but we couldn't seem to work with the dogs and none of us shot well and we were back in town by noon. There had been talk of us going after the geese in a few weeks down at the mouth of Alder swamp, but nobody seemed to want to take charge of making the arrangements and getting us all together, so it never turned into anything. Then, too, when we did meet by accident at Daryl's, say, or the post office, talk was not so much difficult as seemingly not worth the effort or necessary. We had said before that he had gone too far, and without saying it again to each other, we stood by it. And then, there were things to do. The long-range forecast was for a hard winter and there were things to do, things like winterizing our cars and putting up storm windows, like turning our gardens under and raking leaves and banking them against our houses.

THE GOOD LIFE

So I go out to the motor pool to tell my friend Sully about the carrots. We're in the National Guards, and once a month we train at the armory. I'm a cook. While everything's boiling away on this Sunday afternoon, I put a private in charge and go out to the motor pool. My boss at the Red Owl, where I work in produce, is also the mess sergeant and he says the stew needs more carrots and for me to go to the store and get some. I don't argue. I'm glad to get out of the armory and go for a ride. I think Sully'd be glad to go too. I spy his head under a jeep. "Sully," I say. "Want to go for a ride?"

"Where to?" he says.

"Red Owl. I gotta get some more carrots. Meyers gave me the key and says to get some."

"Carrots," Sully says, and rolls out from under the jeep on his creeper.

"I don't care if he says watermelon if I can take a ride," I say. "Where's your sergeant?"

"Furnace room," Sully says. "High man in the poker game."

"Where's your officer?"

"He's one of the pigeons the sarge is plucking." Sully strips off his coveralls and heads for the sink and the GoJo. We're good friends and all because one day he gives me a compliment on the chow. He comes through the line and says he likes the chow. At first I think he's a wise guy, but he means it. So after the line's way down, I go over to where he's eating and sit with him to eat. We get along right from the start.

Outside, we walk over to my Chevy and I fire it up

and we head downtown. The Chevy's not brand new, but I keep it up. People say it looks sharp. It's Sunday, kind of overcast, so I don't feel too bad about having to be at the armory. It's too cool to go to the beach and it kind of looks like rain. We spy a couple of girls on the sidewalk and we sit up straighter in our uniforms. They're only fatigues, but they're still uniforms. We were hoping they were looking. Sully, he's kind of shy. I'm not real good about just walking right up to a girl either. Neither one of us is what you would call a ladies' man. We're both twenty-two, too. Another thing we got in common.

Downtown's got that Sunday look about it. Everything's closed except the movie theater. Lots of windows in the stores got those big smoke-colored plastic liners to keep the clothes on the dummies from getting faded. Hardly nobody on the streets. Next to no traffic. We cruise it anyway and I see how good the Chevy looks in the big windows. Coming up to the light, I stick it in second and let the glass-packs pop off up to the intersection. She sounds good. Sully smiles.

At the light, I hang a right and head down toward the Red Owl. It's all quiet and no cars around except for the maintenance truck parked out front. Red Owl has these professionals that come in on the weekends and mop and polish and dust. I pull up behind their truck and we go up to the door and I open it with the big keyback Meyers wears on his belt. The door opens, and we walk in past the deli and the bakery and head for produce. Then I stop and think.

What I realize is that the cleaning people don't know we're in the store and they're going to be surprised, maybe even scared, when they find out. I'd heard it was a mom-and-pop operation. The polite thing to do, I figure, would be to let them know. We head over to where they are. By the sounds of their Shop-Vac, they're probably in the housewares, soap, and pet-food aisle, so we cut up by the meat counter and swing down that way. They're there, the old man, his wife, and their twenty-some-year-old daughter. The old man's running the vac while his wife and daughter go ahead of him dusting and straightening up the merchandise. The vac's making so much noise they don't hear us right away. We just stand there, waiting for them to notice us. The father's about fifty, wearing a hat and chewing a cigar. The ashes fall into the mop water. He's in his own world, swinging the vac from side to side. His old lady's short and dumpy but with kind of a pretty face. They look Greek or Italian maybe. And then the daughter. She's the first one to turn all the way around, and when she does, I swear to God Sully lets out a groan. She's got this black hair and brown eyes and skin the color of a new cork. She looks up surprised from where she's kneeling by a bottom shelf and then she spins and taps her father on the shoulder. He turns around and shuts off the vac and asks us what we're doing in the store. He's a little excited, but when I tell him what the deal is, he calms down. He switches the vac back on and goes to mopping again. We head back to produce, but Sully's looking back over his shoulder all the way up the aisle. When we get to the bins, he says, "Did you see her?"

"What, I'm blind?" I say.

"Christ," he says.

"Stop dreaming," I tell him, and I pick out a half-dozen packages of carrots. "Let's roll," I tell him. "I gotta feed the troops and KP the mess hall before I can go to the bar. I want to get some drinking in before it closes."

"I gotta see her again," he says. "I'll meet you by the door." Before I can tell him to wake up and see the light, he cuts back toward their aisle again and I head for the door. In a few minutes he's back with a big grin on his face. I ask him what he's smiling about. He says that they just stood there looking at each other, but that she was looking at him too and not just him looking at her. He's not talking too straight. He says that he's going to call her. I tell him that he doesn't even know her name, and he just smiles and points out the window. There's their name right on the side of the old man's panel truck. BENEDETTO'S MAINTENANCE SERVICE, and the home and business phone numbers. Sully's smiling like an idiot, writing the numbers on a matchbook cover. I still don't think he's got the nerve to call her, but on the other hand he did walk back to see her. Still, I think to myself, he'll chicken out.

Back at the armory, after chow I turn the KPs over to a private and head for the bar. Everyone's kind of loose there and we hear all about who were the big winners in the poker game. Sully's sarge cleaned them like a gun rag down a rifle bore. Meyers comes to get his key and says the stew was good, and a bunch of guys standing by us tell me that too. That makes me feel good so I buy a round for all of us. Sully comes up then, so I tell the bartender to get him, too. Sully's grinning like an idiot, and after the bartender gets him his beer, he holds the bottle up for a toast. He can barely talk through his grin. "To victory," he says.

"Victory?" I say. "We're not in a war. We're just in the Guards."

"No," he says, "*my* victory. I called her."

"Benedetto's Maintenance Service? You called that doll? Lemme see your ear where she stuffed the phone. I'll get a medic."

"She said yes," Sully says.

"Yes what?"

"Yes, she'll go out with me. Just for coffee or something at first, but she'll go out. Her main job's a waitress at the Ramada Inn and she said I could come by around ten, when her shift's over tomorrow night, if I wanted to."

"Do you want to?" I say, and I duck as he does the Ali shuffle and puts a few combinations up by my head. "Move like a butterfly, sting like a bee," he says, and then he says, "Put me in, Dundee, I'm ready." I'd never seen him like this before. Later that night out in the parking lot, he walks with me over to the Chevy. It's raining a little like the radio said it might, but it feels good. We stand talking for a minute and then he says, "Terry, what am I going to say to her?"

Her name is Theresa. Theresa-Anne Maria Benedetto. Twenty, single, Catholic, living at home under her old man's roof and rules. Papa isn't too crazy about Sully's being Irish, but being he's Catholic gets him in the door. And the fact that he isn't married or divorced and has a steady job gets him a nod a week later, and after an hour of *bs*-ing in the living room, a glass of homemade dago red up from the basement in a quart milk bottle. Theresa's pasta-mama isn't so easy to warm up. She mostly stands in the kitchen doorway flouring herself or putzing around changing little candles in front of a statue of God's mother in a niche in a wall, all the time with one slant eye on Sully. But after another week, and him and Theresa putting up the summer screens and weeding in the garden, he's invited to go to eleven o'clock mass and then home to a spaghetti dinner with them and their relatives.

I don't see Sully much that summer to talk to, but when I do he's changed, happy. I see him a few times at the armory, but he doesn't stay long after drill is over. One beer and he's out of there to pick up Theresa.

Mostly that summer, I hang around with other guys. I pull my hours at the store, work on cars with some buddies, and go to a few parties. Once in August me'n a girl double-date with Sully and Theresa to a drive-in movie. We bring along a couple of beers and it's a pretty good time until the intermission, when Sully and Theresa go into the concession stand. When they come back, their mood is real tight and they sit in the back whispering hard about Theresa looking at some guy until finally Sully asks me to drive them home. Later, when I drive my date home, she gives me a cool peck and says, "Remind me never to get married." During the rest of the summer I see them together three or four times. They'd be sitting in restaurant windows leaning over a table with their heads together, or sometimes when I'm just cruising, I see them coming out of doorways of stores or the movie theater, Sully holding her arm and guiding her around parked cars or across the street. A couple of times I see them in the theater. One time they're sitting ahead of me and they talk through half the movie. Then they get out of their seats and walk up the aisle past me with their heads down and arguing so loud that anybody ten rows away can hear. After they pass by me, it's hard to get back into the movie.

Later that fall, I see her out with another guy at a dance joint a few miles out of town. I had heard that Sully and her were having serious problems, but then a week later I see them back together again and they act like there was never anything wrong.

In September I see Sully at the armory for Sunday drill. He looks different. He sticks to himself wherever he is, in the motor pool, or on the drill floor, even in the bar. After drill, I go up to him in the bar and I'm going to buy him one and I see he's had quite a few already. And it's not beer. Neither one of us had ever been liquor drinkers because we had both said that we couldn't handle it, but here he is knocking back shots of whiskey without even a chaser. He doesn't look in any too good shape, so I decide against buying him any more.

When I walk up to him, he says, "So, Terry, how the hell's it going? How's your love life? You married yet? Got a house full of kids that look like you? Tell me your love life's story."

"I'm fine, Sully," I tell him. "Say, how's about letting me give you a ride home? You haven't seen the Chevy lately. I got her two-toned."

"You got her two-timed? What, you catch her out with some new hotrod in town?" He laughs but in a kind of sick way.

"What do you say, Sully? I'll give you a ride in the morning to pick up your car before work. Okay?" He just looks at me out of these fogged-up eyes and then grins almost in his old way. "Sure," he says. "And as long as I got a designated driver, I'll have one more of these." To the bartender, he says, "Double this and give one to my chauffeur."

Later in the car he doesn't say too much, except he asks me if I'll drive him past Theresa's house. I do, but the lights are all out and there's only the family's old Plymouth and the truck in the yard. Sully mumbles something I can't make out and then says to take him home.

It's October by now and I'm into other things. I go to camp with a few guys and hunt some grouse. Before I go, I give Sully a jingle to see if he wants to go, but he says no, he doesn't want to leave Theresa. I go, and when I get back, I date the same girl I took to the drive-in movie. She must think that I'm more serious than I am, like Sully maybe, and she keeps the whole night very easy. I kiss her in front of her house when I take her home, but she keeps the kiss as light as a visiting aunt's. I get the message and think to myself, *see you around.*

I hear about the fight from a friend of mine who was there. He's in a roadhouse outside of town and he says Theresa's there at a table with some guy. About an hour later, Sully comes in and stands by the door and just looks around the place. My friend says it looks like Sully'd only come to look around, like maybe he's been to other places before showing up at this one. Sully stares around the room, and when he spies Theresa, he walks over to her and tells her to put her coat on. He's been drinking. She says no and for him to leave, and the other guy stands up. Sully just turns and pastes him and the fight's on. The bartender and a bouncer push them outside and they go at it. Sully's no fighter, but he doesn't quit trying and the other guy really messes him up. When it's over, Theresa's gone. She's taken off crying down the road by herself, and the other guy goes looking for her. My friend drives Sully home.

I see him the next week and he still looks bad. That other guy could really scrap. Sully doesn't say much and I don't either. He just says, "Terry, how's your love life? Got a house full of kids that look like you?" His face is still black and blue on one side and his mouth talks crooked. I say, "Sure, Sully. Don't you?" I don't know what else to say.

He just stands and looks at me. He looks older, like someone who's been away for a long time, only when they come back they look older than the time they've been away. He's skinnier too, not that he was ever fat, but it seems like he's got more skin than he's got use for. After a long time he kind of smiles, but crooked, and says, "How's the Chevy, Terry? Anything new?"

"It's fine, Sully," I tell him. "I got new spoke wheel covers. They look good. Why did you fight him for?"

"I don't know, Terry," he says. "Something happened to me. We were going to get married. She said yes a month ago and now it's off."

"She say why?"

"Who knows?"

"What do you mean?" I ask him.

"It means I'm crazy about her, and when I'm not with her I'm just plain crazy. I don't *know* why. I don't know if *she* does."

"Maybe some time away from each other would be good for both of you," I say. "Me'n a couple of guys are going to deer camp for a few days. Get some deer. Drink some beer. What do you say? We're leaving Sunday night right after drill."

"I don't go to drill anymore," he says. "I quit."

"When did you quit?"

"I just didn't re-up. Theresa just works at the Ramada now and Sunday's her only full day off. I didn't want to miss any of them. Crazy, huh?"

"I don't know," I say. "What about camp?"

"I'll let you know," he says. Then he says, "Thanks."

He doesn't show up at camp, and while I'm there I hear from one of the guys what kind of explains it. Sully can't afford a license or his share of the camp kitty because he doesn't have a job anymore. His boss had canned him for being too moody and having a bad attitude and for showing up smelling like liquor. He had warned him for a couple of weeks and then he let him go. The guy at camp says that Sully respects me too much to be able to tell me. I feel rotten all the time I'm at camp. I even have a perfect shot at a deer and I don't bother. I just holler at it and it takes off. I go back to camp and pack my stuff.

Just before Christmas, the word's around that Theresa's broken it off with Sully and this time for good. They don't date at all, and she's taken up with some assistant manager at the Ramada. He's a real comer and the Ramada's got plans for him. Christmas, he takes Theresa to Hawaii as a present. They stay at a Ramada free of course, but he pops for the whole rest of the trip. Sully says to somebody that he can't compete with that kind of dough. And for good reason, when you think about it. The only job he can land is pumping gas part-time in an all-night station. Minimum wage, and only part-time.

The real trouble is that when he's not at the station, he's in the bars. All afternoon. About six he starts tapering off so that he's sober enough by nine to go to work. He doesn't shave regular and his hair's kind of straggly. Jesus, he used to take pride in his appearance. At least he cared. Now he doesn't seem to care about anything. It makes me feel bad to see him when I remember him the other way.

January and February come dragging in, really crap months in this part of the country. With the holidays over, they're just kind of down months that people try to get through until spring. I see Sully and Theresa once in a while, but not together. She's always with her assistant manager and Sully's always alone. I hear once that Sully makes some threats and they get a court injunction against him that says if he even goes near either of them, he's going to jail. One night I pull into the station where he works for a fill-up. He's outside in this old coat trying to stay warm and gassing up the cars at the pumps. He barely recognizes me, and then he says, "Chevy looks good, Terry." He makes my change then and goes to other cars and doesn't look back or wave or anything. I just figure he's too busy or cold or both, but then driving out, I admit to myself that he's really different. This whole thing took him someplace he can't get back from.

The day after Sully shoots Theresa in the Ramada restaurant, the paper shows a picture of him sitting on the floor holding her head in his lap and people trying to pull him away. There's a wedding in the banquet room, and someone's got this camera. The paper says he just sits there holding her and rocking her and crying, saying her name over and over. The paper says that he had been drinking in a bar all afternoon and that instead of going to work like usual, he goes home and gets a gun and goes to the motel. It says he just walks in and shoots her at a table she's serving. He doesn't shoot anybody else, just her. He shoots her and then he drops the gun and sits down and holds her and keeps saying her name. He's like that when the cops come. It takes three of them to pry his arms from around her. He doesn't resist arrest, and the murder is still under investigation. When I read this, I go to the bathroom and throw up. I don't go out of the house for a couple of days. I don't want to talk to anybody or hear what they got to say. I don't even want to think about it. Sully. And a year ago he can't even say hi to a girl.

He's still in the city jail a month later. The paper says they're bringing in a psychiatrist to see if he's okay to stand trial. He's not nuts. They should ask me. The poor bastard just fell in love with someone. He didn't plan it, but that's the way it turned out. The paper says the court wants to examine his *mental* and *emotional* condition and determine his *motives.* His *motives.* His motive was to be some company for me while I went to get some carrots for a goddamn stew. That could happen to anyone. What I'd like to see is what that psychiatrist has to say about one person wanting another person and that person wanting someone else and why they call it love and why everyone's supposed to be happy to be in it and be all for it.

Last week I see him and it almost kills me. I'm not expecting it. I got the Chevy in a garage downtown for a lube, oil, and filter and I walk up the street to a restaurant to wait until it's ready. I'm walking along looking up at the second stories of these business buildings and there he is. He's just standing in what looks like a hallway with his arms stretched out on this cagelike stuff on the window. He's looking down at me. He doesn't wave and I don't, either. I don't know what to do. We just look at each other. There's no sense trying to talk through that glass, so we don't. He just looks down for a long time and then he shrugs his shoulders and turns and walks away from the window. That's the last time I see him, because in a few days they move him to the county jail about eighty miles away. The paper says the trial won't be for a long time. Legal and psychological *aspects,* the paper says.

I'm still in the Guards. The extra money comes in handy. I think about dating, but who knows. I hear from people that the girl I dated wouldn't mind if I called her again, that she was a little nervous even then because of the Sully-Theresa thing, but I don't know. Who could tell what might happen? I got an uncle who's a bachelor and he doesn't seem too unhappy. He's not grinning all the time, but he's only got himself to spend his money on and he buys a new car every two years and goes fishing and hunting just about whenever he wants. He's just back from deep-sea fishing off the Florida Keys. He asks me to go with him this spring to Canada to fish for walleye. Says a float-plane drops you off right at the dock of your cabin and doesn't come back to get you for a week. Says all you hear is the water and the loons calling and at night the coyotes and the wolves. The good life, he calls it. My ma, his sister, says that he was engaged a long time ago, only it never came off. Says he never talks about it. I hope he stays true to form.

CHILD REARING

My father's death under a bulldozer while he was pushing in a road for a logging company left my mother alone with me and her girlfriends for the first year. A month after he died, she had to go to work as a nurse's aide and so her girlfriends were a mixture of those from the past and new ones she had met at the hospital. They called her often to include her in their plans, but when they did, she just thanked them for the call and sometimes I'd hear her mention my name or the word *time*. Sometimes they would stop at our apartment on Fridays on their way home from work, those from the hospital in their white uniforms and stockings and shoes like she wore. They would come by and kill the hours between five and seven before going home to their husbands or boyfriends. During their stay they sat and drank the wine and beer they had brought and smoked cigarettes, their feet propped on our coffee table or tucked up under themselves. While they talked, I would try to get into the bathroom around their visits there and get ready for my own weekend. After a few beers my mother might say something like, "Lyle's the man of the house now," or, "We're a team, aren't we, Lyle?" Sometimes when I wasn't in a mood for answering and stuck my attention on getting ready, she would say things like, "Who is she tonight, Lyle? Anybody I know?" From the bathroom I once heard her say that my father's death, even though it was an accident, was his fault *in a way,* because he didn't always have to run a bulldozer, which was so dangerous, that he could have tried to get a job where things like that had less of a chance of happening. By the time I would leave, she and her girlfriends would be a little bit drunk, but not in a serious way. They would tell her to keep her chin up and that when she was ready she should *just call.* That God didn't mean for anybody to live alone. Sometimes in the driveway, if we were leaving at the same time, one of them would give me a hug or a slap on the ass and say, "Now, don't you do anything I wouldn't do," or, "If you can't be good, be careful."

My father's death had left us with no insurance, no income, and dim prospects. But he and my mother had loved each other and she had followed him from job to job in one part of the country or another with no more concern for a permanent home than a bird.

At eighteen, I was half her age and with a few adjustments on both our parts, we could go with each other to some of the same places. In bars where my father had been known I was made to feel welcome, but I could not get served. In bars where they had not been known, if the crowd was big enough and the lighting was right, at times I could get served. And so on some Friday or Saturday nights we would go out for a supper and then maybe do some shopping where there were sales and spend the rest of the night going from places like the Miner's bar to The Pines and end up at The Drift, where they had the best music, locals, but good, who played, my mother said, so that you could dance without ending up in the ER with a dislocated hip. In these places we would order nuts and chips and pour from a pitcher of beer at a back table at the edge of the light from the dance floor.

All of the men from the bar saw her, and more than a few would come over and ask her to dance. She was always polite in ways that I couldn't be sure weren't flirting, but she made it clear that she did not want to dance. She would say things like, "I only dance with my fella here," or, "My date wouldn't like it." They would look at me and size up the relationship and back away into the crowd. Sometimes she would look after them but not say anything and then it wouldn't be too long that she'd ask me if I felt up to dancing with an old lady.

She was as at home on a dance floor as she must have been at sixteen. She would slide out from the table and into the light and by the time I moved out to her, she would already be swaying with one arm lifted and the wrist out to fit my shoulder, her body gone with the music. She danced absently, guiding without really leading, and sometimes sang in a low voice along with the music. She was small in her clothes and to my mind even now was without thought as to how she looked or who was looking. At those times she seemed not twice my age but just my age or younger, and it could have been that I was the parent and she the child and not the other way around.

She needed looking after. I was willing to do it for a while, but I had my own life, which just then was taken up with hunting season and trying to graduate from high school and spending some time with my friends. That and pumping gas twenty hours a week to make my car payments. No earth-shaking matters, but they were mine and managed to use up what hours I wasn't sleeping. What I had left went to her, and when she was ready I would be willing to give the job to someone more her own age.

After the first year, she and her girlfriends decided the matter for me. It didn't come in any special way so as to tell it immediately from the time when she was not yet ready. It was more the tone in her and her girlfriends' conversations as they sat in our living room on those Friday evenings. One woman in particular, a large blonde who worked in OB with the babies, said that my mother was still young enough to have more children, at least one. My mother winked at me. It wasn't clear altogether, but something had happened or was happening. A time had passed or a corner had been turned and now that we were on the other side of whatever it had been, it was time to be getting on.

The first of the men to appear was one that I had seen with my father in his work, a widower older than her by about twenty years. He sat at the kitchen table on their second date and wore on his face the grief he felt over being too old and out of the running. He just looked at her as if she were an unattainable prize that an accident of time had too far distanced from him. He stood up from the table shaking his head. "I'm going to leave now," he said, "so that you just remember me as old and not as an old fool."

There were others. One came with an appraising eye and, when he thought nobody was looking, surveyed the household goods and her car in the driveway. He did everything but count on his fingers. Another allowed one evening, when he didn't know I could hear, that marriage was in his plans for the future but not children, and that the military service was a fine place for a boy just out of high school with no special goals. My mother asked him what in the hell he was talking about and within a few minutes I heard his car start up outside. Others, too, made tracks doggedly to the door, but these she turned away out of hand. They wore what they wanted too openly on their faces and looked as if they didn't have much time.

And then she met Russell. He was a construction foreman for an out-of-town crew that was adding a new wing to the town's small hospital. One day he had stepped through an opening in a wall into a hallway where my mother was pushing a food steamer. He had stood staring foolishly at her and holding a bloodied finger in his other hand. Twice that week they took their coffee breaks together and on Friday night he was at our door.

He was a big, ruddy-colored man who looked uncomfortable in dress clothes. His hands were large and when he took one of mine in his to shake it I could feel its slick surfaces, smoothed by years of working with concrete and steel, in the way that grinding sea-sands polish rock. His grip was loose, as if my hand were a small animal and he feared hurting it. When he finished shaking it lightly, he set it free and sat in the kitchen waiting for her to get ready. When she returned to us pretty and ready, he moved carefully around her as if she might break. As they were leaving, she asked me my plans for the evening and I told her. He nodded in such a way as to say that they sounded reasonable, as if maybe he had agreed to such plans before. They took her car that night. The company pickup he had driven into town was parked at the curb and when I looked into it I saw why they had taken hers. Except for where he sat, the rest of the seat was taken up with things from his work.

Russell lived in a motel that had kitchenette units for men like him, who would be in the area for longer stays. It was an old motel, small, just on the edge of town where the town's streetlights left off and the road went on until the next town, an hour or so away. There was a gravel driveway across the front of the motel, and more than half of it was taken up by trucks from Russell's company and some over-the-road rigs. Every weekend and some weekdays, she and Russell were together. Around me he was polite and seemed to consider my feelings in matters that concerned me. For all of that, he never asked my permission and never acted as if I were older than I was. We were just two men, one older and one younger, in the same house with a woman and we made room for each other.

This was in the fall, and now that she had someone with her, I went about my business of trying to get through my senior classes and working and doing some dating of my own. Like the boys in that small town, the girls knew that there were other places in the world and other, maybe better, prospects. We dated at random, and in the absence of those other further prospects, we had our times with each other. Most dates ended up in a parking session west of town by a paid-out quarry.

Sometimes on my dates I would see her car parked at restaurants or in front of the movie theater. A few times I saw Russell and her going in or out of bars. One Saturday night when I was out riding around with some of my buddies, we saw a crowd of cars parked in front of the Drift and we could hear the C&W music pouring out the door. The place was packed, so we thought that if we played our cards right, we might be able to get served. We went in and worked our way through the crowd to a table in back. The light was dim there and we were hoping for some luck. A little ways away from us, I saw Russell and her sitting by themselves.

They seemed deep in a conversation and at times she would look at him and smile the way I remembered her smiling at my father. While I watched, they got up and danced to "Your Cheatin' Heart," and when it was over they stayed on the floor holding on to each other while the band made some changes for the next song. He held her with his hands low on her hips. While he held her like that, she looked beyond his shoulder and saw me sitting with my friends. For a long moment we looked at each other in a way that felt to me like spying and then she turned and his hands rode up. The music started then and she went back to dancing. I told my buddies that we didn't have a chance of getting served and that we should get out of there.

After she started dating Russell, her girlfriends didn't come around on Friday evenings anymore. Sometimes she didn't come right home after work because she and Russell had stopped off somewhere. When she came home later, she would be all excited about where they were going that night and she would fly around the house getting ready and in an hour be gone again. Some nights I would be back from my night out before she went out again and I would hear her play the radio loud. It wasn't worth it to mention the noise to her or that in the morning I had to get up for work. Since Russell, she was in a lifted mood and I didn't want to chance spoiling it.

Sometimes Russell would come home after work with her and wait while she got ready. While she did, he and I would talk at times but never about anything very specific. How was school? How was work? Sports. Such topics allowed us to fill what would otherwise have been dead, awkward air and I think that we were both glad for them. There wasn't much about me that she probably hadn't already told him. I was a senior and I didn't know what I was going to do when I graduated. What more was there to tell? That left me asking him questions. He answered them but didn't volunteer much else. He had been in construction work all his life and operated out of a central office downstate in Detroit. It was good work with good pay but without much of a home life to it. His next job, depending on how the bidding went, would be in either Tacoma or Cleveland. That was the business. You never knew for sure. I didn't get all this information at the same time. This much I gathered during the course of a couple visits. Without coming right out and asking him what his intentions were where my mother was concerned, I had to be satisfied with what I got. Once when I asked my mother, she stared at me and said, "Ask him if you're so nosy. Can't we just have a good time without you getting all serious?" It was the first time she had snapped at me since my father had died.

In late November she and Russell came home with a half-dozen boxes and bags in their arms. They were full of clothes and she tore into them and started laying dresses and slacks and shoes and a coat over the back of the couch. She was flushed from both the weather and the excitement and she had never looked prettier. She hugged Russell and turned to me with her arms still around his neck. "Russell took me shopping," she said. "It's the first time I've shopped and it wasn't a sale in a year. Aren't they beautiful, Lyle? Don't you love them?" She picked up the coat and held its collar up to her face and let the rest of it fall the length of her body. "Lyle, look at this," she said. "Have you ever seen anything so beautiful?"

I was waiting up for her when she came in that night. The room was half-dark, and when she came through the door, she did not see me sitting in a corner chair in the living room. She went to the closet and turned on the light and took the new coat off. Before she hung it up, she smoothed it down with her hand and settled it carefully on the hanger. She stood there for a moment in the glow of the light and gazed at the coat. The light was small through the closet door and in its dim shaft her eyes were bright and her color was high. Before she closed the door, she picked up a sleeve of the coat in one hand and rubbed it lightly with the other. She was very happy, but I had to say something. I said, "How much did he pay for all of that?" I had surprised her and she turned to locate me in the room. I hadn't meant to, but I had spoiled it for her. "Why?" she said.

"I'm just wondering," I said.

"What difference does it make?" she said. She came across the room and stood in front of me. She was angry now and her voice was flat. "Do you want to see the bill?" she said.

"No," I said. "I was just wondering. We don't know much about him. It's only been five weeks."

"Who's counting?"

"Nobody's counting," I said. "But all we know is that he's from Detroit and he's going to Tacoma or Cleveland next. That's not much to go on."

"For who?" she said. "Not much for who to go on?" She sat down then on the couch across from me. She slipped off her new high-heel shoes and placed them next to each other and lined up the toes. "I've still got the boxes," she said. "I've only worn three of the things. I'll take it all back in the morning. Will that make you happy?"

"It's not a question of making me happy," I said. "It's just we don't know . . ."

"*We?*" she said. She stood up then. "I'm going to bed."

"Wait a minute," I said, but she had already turned and disappeared through her bedroom door. She closed it behind her. When I got up in the morning, she had already left for work.

We were quiet with each other that week. She and Russell ate out three or four times and at night either I didn't come in or she didn't until the other was asleep. When we were in the house together, I didn't mention the clothes again and she didn't return them. At the end of that week, she did not come home on Friday night.

I waited for her until mid-morning on Saturday and then grabbed my gear and headed out to my buddy's dad's deer camp, about forty miles out of town. As I was leaving, I passed Russell's motel. Her car was parked among the trucks.

By the time I got to the camp, it was close to noon and the guys were having beer with their lunch. I wasn't in the mood for an all-afternoon session, so I took my gun and headed out cross-country to a stand of hardwoods a mile or so away. The day was clear, but the sky was only half-high in a thin haze, the sun pale and low to the south. The dark, tall oaks lifted out of shallow wells of snow and their bare branches let down shadows on the bright ground. I had nothing more in mind than to spend the afternoon taken up with something other than her and Russell. It felt good to be carrying the gun.

At about three o'clock I came upon his tracks. They were broad and splay-toed, fresh and clear in the new snow. He was an old swamp buck up from the lowland cedars for the rut. Mixed in with his tracks were others, smaller, probably those of does that were traveling with him or that he was pushing ahead to sound for him. I followed them for about a quarter-mile and then I saw him downwind about a hundred yards from me, the does standing dumbly by as he lifted his heavy head to sniff at the scarred bark of trees where he or another buck had left his mark. He was huge, high in the shoulders and broad-chested. His years in the swamps had darkened him to match the depths of his shadow on the snow. He walked a few feet away from the tree and urinated and returned to the does, which nosed into the snow, mindless of anything but him. Then he moved off from them a ways and disappeared into the trees and I couldn't see him.

In about five minutes I heard him snort behind me. He was somewhere back there and he snorted again and then again to call them away. Snapping their heads up, their ears pricked, they flagged and broke for him.

I tracked him until about four-thirty and then I saw him for a second time. He was far up ahead of me on a small rise, moving slowly with them through a stand of birch. He stopped once and put his head down and by the time I got to where he had been, I saw where he had been pawing into one of his old scrapings in the snow, dragging his hooves through it and opening it up to the ground beneath. The snow down the side of the scraping was yellow. A little while later I saw him for the third and last time, on higher ground still, now as dark as the oaks he browsed through. He moved at his ease, the foolish does at his flanks, the three of them caught up in the simple rhythms of the rut. We spied each other from a hundred yards out and I felt the uselessness of my carbine. I needed at least a 30.06 and a longer barrel. He lifted his wide rack up and, turning it toward me, he stamped once and trotted a few feet forward and stopped. He took his time, as if he had all of it that he needed, as if he could smell on the soundless wind not only my scent but also my youth and inexperience. He looked down at me through the trees' spread shadows, his rack's span lifted, motionless. For a long time we stood in the graying woods as late afternoon came down and we watched each other. Finally, as if to signal an end to it, he stamped again and threw his head and snorted. Then he turned his back on me and trotted off with his does into the woods.

I went back to camp that night and drank too much beer and spent the night there.

When I got back to the apartment in the morning, she was waiting for me. She was at the kitchen table drinking coffee with a half-full ashtray in front of her. She had been crying and looked like she had not had much sleep. Part of me felt bad and part of me didn't. I said nothing and was heading for my bedroom with my gear when she said, "Where in the hell have you been?"

"Hunting," I said.

"Hunting? I've been up all night over you. You couldn't leave a note? Don't they teach you to write in that school?" When I kept going toward my bedroom, she shouted, "You get back here. I'm not through talking to you." I dropped my gear on the floor and walked back to her. "What else?" I said.

"What do you think what else? I stay up all night over you and you breeze in here like there's nothing to talk about." She lit another cigarette and pulled her bathrobe around her. "Since when do you start staying out all night and not telling me?"

"How about you?" I said. "Don't bother telling me. I saw your car yesterday morning."

"Don't bother telling *you,*" she said. She put her

cigarette out in the ashtray and stabbed at loose sparks. She moved the butt around, rubbing all the sparks out while I waited for what she had to say next. Finally, she said, "Where I was Friday night is my business."

"And it's not mine?" I said.

"No, it's not."

"Since when?" I said.

"Since the day I was the one who gave birth to you. That's since when. I'm your mother, in case you've forgotten."

I was going to say that lately it was not hard, but I held it back. Instead, I said that he was going to be moving on soon, in case she didn't know. That that was the nature of his business. After thinking about it, I went on to tell her all of it. "And I'm damn sure that he's married," I said.

"*You are?*" she said.

"Yeah I am."

"And what makes you so sure?"

"Things he says, the way he acts. He's been around a family before."

"And that bothers you? Is it that or me with any man besides your father?"

"It's not that," I said.

"He's every bit as good a man as your father."

"You ought to know," I said. She was out of her chair then in a second and her hand was across my face. She was crying and with her slap I almost did too. "What the hell do you know," she said. "You think you know everything and you don't know anything. Why don't you get the hell out of here? Just get the hell out."

She went into her bedroom and slammed the door. I slammed the door of the apartment when I left.

I rode around town for a while and then went to a restaurant downtown and sat at the counter drinking coffee and trying to think my way through. The street was quiet, with only Sunday traffic. In about a half hour I saw Russell's pickup go by, and I left money on the counter and went out.

He was at the second light one street before his motel by the time I got into my car. I followed him, and when he turned in, I went on past his place and drove on the two-lane out of town for a ways. Four or five miles out, I pulled into a camp road and turned around and headed back to town. His pickup was there when I pulled into the driveway and parked by an over-the-road rig.

When he came to the door, he was in his work clothes and putting heavy glasses back into a leather case clipped to his shirt pocket. Papers covered with figures and blueprints were on the bed and a small table next to it. He stepped aside and invited me in. While I moved past him into the room he said, "You're a hard man to find, son. Your mother was worried sick."

"I went hunting," I said, and waited while he moved toward the bed and started gathering up the papers to put them on the table. "Bed's the most comfortable thing in this Taj Mahal," he said. "I'll make you some room to sit."

"Don't bother," I said.

"Then I hope you don't mind if I sit," he said. "I been up driving until four this morning. You should have left your mother word. She's had quite a bit for one year, and she worries easy."

"I know that," I said. When I didn't sit down, he pushed the chair he was going to sit on back to the table by the bed. We stood a few feet apart. "Last night I must've driven fifty miles of back roads. This place doesn't have a whole lot of paved ones. Can I ask you where you were?"

"I went hunting," I said. "And then I decided to stay the night."

"You do any good hunting?"

"I saw one."

"Get a shot?"

"Close," I said, "but he moved off."

"They'll do that," he said. He paused for a moment and said, "What's on your mind?"

"You," I said. "And her."

"Like what?" he said.

"Like Friday night and whether you're married or staying or what the deal is."

"What do you think the deal is?"

"I don't know," I said.

"Well," he said, "I've been married, but I think I told you that there's not much of a home life to this line of work. Would it bother you if I was?"

"She needs something better than that."

"I won't argue with you there," he said.

"What are you going to do about it?"

"It's already been done. I'll be in Tacoma within the month."

"Does she know?"

"As of Friday night."

"Did you ask her to go with you?"

"No."

"Why not?" I said.

"I'm not what she needs," he said.

"But you needed her."

"We needed each other," he said. Then he said, "Look, Lyle. Someday you'll understand this."

"I think I do now," I said.

"You do, do you?" he said. "Then I guess we'll have to go with that. Maybe it's all we're going to get. Did you get what you wanted by coming here?"

"I don't know why I came here," I said.

"Not knowing isn't the worst thing, I wouldn't think," he said. "Strikes me knowing and not caring's probably the worst."

During the following week, I went to school and work and left the two of them to themselves. She and I said hello and goodbye at the apartment, but even that was not too often because she spent most of her time with Russell. A couple of nights that week she did not come home again. Saturday was the last day of hunting season, so when she didn't come home on Friday night, I headed out to camp in the morning. By noon I was in the woods and I spotted the buck's tracks again. They weren't as clear in the light, falling snow, but they were his. By this time there were no more scrapings and he was traveling alone.

His tracks took me up into the hardwoods in early afternoon and twice I could see where he had lain down and rested. He could afford to rest because he had paid attention to the wind and I hadn't. Once I glimpsed him in the oaks about eighty yards out, walking with his head up and turning. He caught me on the wind and flagged and disappeared over a rise, heading back toward the swamp. This time I checked the wind and paralleled him for about a quarter-mile, staying downwind. He was slow but alert, and without his tracks to guide me, I had to depend on small sightings of him through the trees as we both moved off the high ground. Then, when I crossed the narrow spine of an esker and looked down the other side, I spotted him at the swamp's edge, stopped.

In front of him lay a long line of heavy cedars, low and dense where the swamp began and the open country left off. On the cedar line's open edge, the new snow weighed the trees down and he was feeding along their skirts. He was close enough for me to see the snow clinging to his rack. I checked his movements and made my moves whenever his head was down.

I held the bead of my sight on the dark part behind his shoulder while he fed at the cedars, the snow shaking down out of the branches. When he lifted his head to test the wind, I froze but kept the dark part of him on my bead. The last time he lowered his head I started again to tighten my finger on the trigger, but after a while, I realized that I wasn't going to shoot. I thought about that until gradually whatever had been in me to shoot him went completely out of me and the tears came that hadn't come with my mother's slap. I thumbed the hammer and put the gun down. When I could see again, he was gone.

When I drove back into town in the evening, the window in the Drift was steamed and the neon sign in it was blurred. Her car was parked out front. I looked around for her and Russell, but I only saw her sitting at a table with some of the women from the hospital and their men. They were all talking, but she didn't seem to be involved in it very much. She had her chair turned and was watching the people on the dance floor. I went over to her table and pulled a chair up. She smiled a little when I sat down. I asked her where Russell was.

"He left at noon for Detroit," she said. "Next week they'll fly him out to Tacoma."

"So soon?" I said. "I didn't think it'd be this quick."

"He didn't either, but they called."

"Did you want to go with him?"

"In a way," she said, "but not really. He asked me to this morning."

"He asked you to?"

"Are you surprised?"

"Not really," I said. Then I said, "Yeah, in a way I guess."

"He told me that you went to see him."

"Yeah, I went," I said.

"And?"

"I don't know," I said.

"You don't, either?" she said.

For a while we sat and watched the people dance and we didn't say anything. There was nothing to say because too much had been said already, and done, things we'd had no control over. Something in me hitched up my breath and when it went out of me I felt quiet.

With the music and all the people dancing, the bar was very warm and with the windows steamed we couldn't see outside. Someone in her group of friends said something funny and she turned to smile. When she faced around to look at me, she was still smiling but it wasn't at the remark. It was a slow, steady smile that said it was all right now, and what do you do with a life that comes at you in such strange ways? She didn't say any of this. What she said was, "Were you hunting today?"

"Yeah," I said, "but I didn't see anything."

"Lyle," she said. "He's a good man. Like your father. What do you think? Could you dance with an old lady?"

Then she was out of her chair. Moving but not yet dancing, she worked her way out onto the floor and down the edge of the dance crowd. I tried to follow her, but the couples kept swinging out and for a moment I lost her. Then I spied her in a clearing in the crowd. She had moved into it and with the small space around her she had turned and was waiting for me. Among all the people she was very small and at times it was difficult to see her. While I made my way to her, she kept her eyes on me and when I reached her she was already taken by the music, her one arm lifted, her wrist out to fit my shoulder.

SWIMMING

Sinking, I drift down faster than I had imagined or feared, through water and the strata of years, my small son's death grip around my neck, his knees, a jockey's, spurring my sides, the two of us riding my short breath to the floor of the Municipal Commemorative Park pool. Though my efforts to keep us both afloat seem to take ages, actually it has been only moments since, in a weighted panic, I gulped half the air we needed and sank to the bottom. Above us, legs with their heads in air pump and pedal as if oxygen were a given, and directly overhead a body floats. The water muffles and scatters sounds while I siphon swallowed air and work to free his fingers knotted at my throat. He squirms on my back and digs in tighter, either from panic or not knowing that the game is over, and I roll to my side and settle on the bottom. There I pry his fingers loose and suddenly he is all arms and legs bubbling up to the bright air. With a push I am right behind him and break the surface, where he is already twisting away and dog-paddling toward the shallow end and his mother, who looks up from her book with a worried look for him and a question for me. From his stand, an alerted lifeguard, sunglassed and Noxzema-nosed, scolds down at me. Light-headed, eating air, I see that we were never in danger, that he was there all the while and watching. Besides, this is a city park with banked flower beds, security patrols, and a coral-colored band shell—civilized, tame—not the treacherous waters of Michigan's Upper Peninsula lakes and basins and paid-out quarries. Avoiding stares from my wife and the lifeguard, I wade to the shallow end and sit on a bench.

* * *

My father was not especially athletic, neither by build nor inclination. He was middle-sized, slight, and not to be named by what he did for a living. By turns he had been a woods worker, mason's helper, roofer, truck swamper, lumber piler, and farm laborer, all for short durations, all seasonal. His school years remain a mystery to me, but I have never heard of sports being connected with them. In his adult years he followed no sport, was no team's fan. His habit, however, was to come home from work to eat a light supper, mostly liquids, and head for the nearest body of water, weather permitting, to swim. *Weather permitting* meant from the first days in spring when the waters warmed to the last days in late fall when they seized and grew a skin of ice. Also, he was able, when I was very young, to swim with me on his back.

The first time he tried this was a sultry July night. When he wasn't home by dark, my mother sent me to the public beach on a lake a block away to look for him. I called, and when he didn't answer, I kicked off my shoes and waded out up to my ankles. When he didn't answer, I called louder. When he still didn't answer I called again, my voice sharpened to a yelp. By now I was knee deep and inching out. And then, his head grazing my leg, his slicked hair tight like an otter's, he was grinning at me. "Looking for somebody?" he said.

"Yeah," I said. "Mom wants you to come home."

"Yeah," he said. "We will. I want to try something first. Get on my back." He crouched down into the water.

"Mom wants you to come home," I said again, already trying to slide up him in the dark. His back felt like a washboard with skin. "Up higher," he said, and I struggled to gain a hold, finally pushing my knees into the hollows beneath his ribs and tangling my fingers in the cup below his throat. He eased out deeper until the water began to lift us, hung there for a moment, then pushed off the bottom in a surge and we were swimming. At first his strokes were sharp and deep, his body turning to drive all its power into the pulling arm until, seeming to tip the earth, he made what felt not like an adjustment in his body but rather like a change in the water itself, so that it did what he would have it do. Then he settled into an orchestration of muscle and water and air that carried us out into the night toward no destination that I could see. Tight to me, the machinery of his body moved in flawless time and, rocked by its regularity, were it not for my fear, I could have slept. Gradually, the fear left me and I saw where we were headed. Glowing on the water in front of us a Clorox bottle bobbed, marking the swimming area's outer limits. We swam toward it and then past it and then, many strokes out, we turned and headed back, our return signaled by his yips of pleasure that skipped across the water.

On shore, in small, quick, one-legged dances, he snapped the water from his ears and, bending at the waist, let his long hair fall forward like weeds. Then he flipped it all back and fingered the lank strands to his head. Having made this adjustment to land living, he took me by the hand and we headed for home. Once, seeming to comment more to the night around us than to me, he said, "Damnit, I *knew* I could do that!" After a few minutes of silent walking, he said, "Damn," again and threw a rock against the side of a trash can. Walking in his bathing suit, he carried his clothes and shoes rolled up in a towel. I walked quietly at his side, wet and still fully clothed.

He didn't always swim alone. At times he could entice Mother and us three kids down to the lake, any lake, and there we would have our supper, which he cooked with much fanfare over guttering-out charcoal. Mother sat on a blanket he had spread for her, the guest of honor, by his proclamation; she who could do no cooking, who should sit and *enjoy.* When supper was over, he would pull us all toward his shallow waters. He cavorted for us on the loose sand and lured us from our squabbles and huddling towels and small alliances. One by one he drew us off the beach and toward his antics. Tentative, testing, we waded out, the evening waters chilling our legs, thoughts of water on our bellies holding us back. Taking care to not splash, he moved among us, sleek, cajoling, wooing us from dry to wet until finally he said, *Now,* and we dove, and the cold water turned warmer and we cruised his lake bottom wide-eyed and brave and then rose up to him. We swarmed him and, finding handholds on his neck and arms, we dragged him shoreward, where he lolled with us in the inch-high waters.

Other times Mother and one or two of us would follow in a rowboat as he took his evening swim. While Mother trolled over the stern for fish and I sat squared in the center seat, seeking balance between the awkward oars, he swam at the boat's side in long, supple, splashless strokes, head turning, shoulders lightly lifting. We glided past early-evening fishermen and cottagers on their docks and small beaches. Side by side we pulled past quiet bays, and at times he talked, to Mother mostly, about work and quarterly reports, supply and demand, unfamiliar forces that found and confused him yearly, leaving him stunned. When we reached the other end of the lake, he would walk with Mother for a while down the beach while I waited by the boat.

That summer he had worked in a sawmill, and when the contracted timber had been cut and milled and there was no more for him to stack into piles, he left us. He didn't write for a week, and when he did, it was a few printed sentences on a postcard that our mother passed around the supper table for us to read. His new job was as a woods worker in the western end of the Peninsula.

He would be home in a day or two to help pack. The front side of the card, in colors of bright blue and green, showed a small, smooth lake surrounded by trees, once pointed up in the air and once, upside down, reflected in the water.

Our new home, a shallow socket at the base of glacial rubble, was a stalled copper-mining town. Over the years it had been broken by market failings, union strikes, and company reprisals. A symbol of its luck stood in the center of town: an unused smelter, completed for its grand opening in 1945, closed on that same day. V-E had been declared. Years later, as we drove into town pulling everything we owned in a rented trailer, its broken windows and peeled paint loomed ahead of us.

A logging truck came each morning and took our father up into the wooded hills miles out of town and returned him at dark, red and raw, smelling of sawdust and pitch and gasoline from the chain saws. Frostbite whitened his ears and fingers, and icy snow, packed in his sleeves, bloodied his wrists. The skin on his chin and forehead froze and peeled and froze again, and each night mother salved it with heavy cream.

He swam very little that winter. The work in the woods and the early evening dark left him with little time or energy at the end of a day. Only a few times did he go to the high school swimming pool in a tall, cold vaulted room where the winter night blackened the windows. Once a week it was open to the public, but not many people used it. He would go there and change into his swimming suit and walk out to the pool, its long lanes shimmering but still, a light steam rising.

On the walls hung life rings and poles and cork floats, signs of daytime activity, but now, at night, dim and silent, the pool lay uninviting, its gently undulating surface moved by motors deep in a subterranean pump room. On tiptoe he would quickly cross the cold floor, slapping his arms, and lean to a stop at the pool's edge, staring down. Then something grew slowly in the room's chill, grew until it came to replace the cold inhospitality of that stone-and-tile chamber. It flattened goose bumps and eased the stiffness from his body, which straightened and then arched over the water. In the air he would let out a resounding *whoop!* and echoes rolled down the walls even after he had pulled his first yards of water behind him. Then, for an hour or two, he stroked laps down the pool's length, curling a continuous wave.

That winter, for the second and last time, he swam with me on his back. I was eight years old, chicken-chested, thin skin on a hollow frame. At his request I slid up his back at the pool's shallow end and floundered there for a moment until the water had me and then, buoyant, I floated into place and found mooring on his ribs and neck. He moved off into the water and for the length of the pool fought against the weight I had gained. A few yards from the wall at the deep end, we started to go down. He struggled there until finally his arms thrashed the water by my head and then we were under and I let go. I floated to the wall, and when he came up next to me, he spoke in a submerged voice, his chin still in the water. I couldn't understand the words, but then he turned and kicked off the wall and was gone.

The following summer he awoke to find that his job, as if on wires, had been pulled away from him. He stood at the end of our walk waiting for the truck to pick him up, and when it didn't, he came back into the house. Someone on the phone told him that there was a decline in housing starts and a surplus of lumber. He was, the voice said, eligible for unemployment checks.

He crisscrossed the county looking for work. Following tips and rumors, he worked his way out of town and into outlying villages, stopping to ask in the open doors of gas stations and warehouses. Farther out, sometimes across the line and into Wisconsin, he stood at the tailgates of trucks being loaded in fields and gave a hand with crops while he asked if there was any work to be had.

Evenings, he would return home and after supper spend time around the house looking after us children and talking to Mother. The day's heat carried into evening and, with it, the sensation of something pending, held back, waiting for its moment. He would grow restless and move from room to room until finally he would start putting his swim things into a bag and look questioningly at Mother. Her answer, polished in the grooves of routine, was a nod and the words, "Don't be too late."

Water in that harsh country was dark, having leaked slowly from hills and spiny eskers to stand deep in old stone quarries and rock pockets. Pines on the higher ground and lowland cedars ringed the lakes, adding depth and shadows. He was drawn that summer to these deep waters, preferring to swim late at night, when lakes were just black plates under the stars. He would come back wet, late, his face wearing a look of apology, his voice full of distance. In his mind, an idea must have been forming; of lakes becoming rivers, rivers opening into larger lakes, they in turn flowing into seas and oceans, giving him, finally, a vision of the wide world, wet, loosely girdled by water. Or perhaps he may have simply felt buoyed up and able to swim forever.

Now, in the evenings, he began to swim longer and later; during the daytime he swam in air.

In a field behind our house he tied pulleys and ropes and a pair of sand-filled gallon cans to the lowest branches of two pines. To the base of the trees he dragged a picnic-table bench. Lying full-length on it, facedown over one end, his hands looped in the rope's loose ends, he swam, working against the weights. From our kitchen window we could see his arms rising and curving down, sometimes a glimpse of his back, so that he seemed to be swimming over the foot-high grass. In weeks, small muscles, moles, moved in the skin on his arms.

Mid-summer, following one of his leads, we moved from Michigan to a farm loosely fenced into northern Wisconsin fields. We only traveled a hundred miles or so, but in that distance thick woods thinned, hills flattened, and rivers widened. Fields flowed in swells of bright then paling grasses. In these contours, water was truer to the earth's curve. Lacking deep places to stand, meandering through fields of stolid cows and tractors inching over miles, it appeared to be loosed in its flowing—shallow, lithe, and traveling light. Slowing at village limits, it swelled and fattened to grace local parks until, out of town, it ventured cross-country to duck under bridges, divide around small islands, then, folding in foam, pour together again, streaming south. As he stepped out into the yard of the farmer who had hired him, Father said to Mother that a man could be lucky here.

Our house was at the back of the farmer's property, a small one he had for families, like ours, who might need it. A month later, as Father walked into the kitchen in the middle of an afternoon, he said, "Last hired, first fired," and dropped his hat on the table. Mother was sitting there drying dishes. "How in the world do you plant the wrong crop?" he asked her.

"I don't know what you mean," she said.

"He planted the wrong crop and the market won't buy it, and he can see already that he won't be needing me. Can't afford me."

"How much time do we have?" Mother said. She had left off drying a plate and sat folding the dish towel into small squares and creasing each edge with the flat of her hand.

"Not long," Father said.

His next job carried us downstream through the Fox River Valley for forty or fifty miles. We rode through softwood trees and river-scrub on a two-lane blacktop that clung to the river's stretched *S*s and lazy sways, its traffic seeming to take its notions of speed from the slow, wide water. The Fox seemed in no hurry, having just left Lake Winnebago and going only to Lake Michigan's Green Bay. Farms grew right down to the river bank, but this was mostly store country, those that sold what the farmers grew or needed and those that sold what the river gave up. Others seemed to sell the river itself by way of signs saying EAT ON THE RIVER, SLEEP ON THE RIVER, FISH, PLAY, LIVE ON THE RIVER.

Three days a week he watered and fed the animals in the holding barns at a farmers' cooperative and shoveled and dumped the manure into steaming piles behind the barns. He also cut the grass around the front offices and in general kept up a tidy appearance. On weekends, he only had to water and feed the animals, an hour's work each day, and we children helped him. With no bosses around, we zoomed through the sun-slatted barns, skidding in the straw, and pushed buckets into the cows' big, chewing faces. His job on the other two days was one that he only described to Mother. He didn't know that some of us children could hear. He told her that on these days he went and stood in his oldest clothes just inside the door of a shed to the back of the cooperative's land. He waited there with a mallet in his hands, and as cows were led up a ramp and through a small door, he hit them as hard as he could behind the ear. After they went down he would watch them and, if they moved, hit them again. When he came home on these days he was especially quiet and he stood at the kitchen sink for a long time, washing his hands and arms in elbow-deep, soapy water. Then, after a light supper, he headed for the river.

Mother drove the car with us children ranged along the backseat. We dropped him off in a driveway alongside a gas station, getting out to watch him walk barefoot through a small, tin jungle of gas cans, kerosene drums, and rusted car parts, through grease-stiffened grass down a treeless path to the river. Its edges were silty and he picked his way out like a cat, lifting a leg and shaking it, making his way past floating lily pads and into the swirling edgewaters. Past them, he slipped through the sudsy sidestream, waded to his thighs, leaned into the current until it caught him, and then went with it. The trick, he had told us, was to go with it yet swim at the same time, to be in control but let the river do the work. Like this, he would move gradually out into the middle of the wide river, where the current ran stronger and deeper, and we would go back to the car and follow him for miles, picking him up downriver in the next little town.

From the road we could catch glimpses of him in the mid-river waves. That far out he was hard to see, but his head would appear sleek, a shiny dot in the small whitecaps. Around the corners of houses, past sloping lawns, through the smoke of backyard barbecues and small knots of people gathered in yards, we paced him in his swift journey down, all of us craning to see him first, screaming our sightings to each other. Behind a Dairy Queen, our treats in hand, we waited as he made his way up a river path and toward the car.

He did that a half-dozen times that summer, each time swimming a little longer and leading us in the car a little farther down the road. At the end of his swim was always a treat of ice cream for us as we listened to his excited talk. Then one day, as all of us stood in the parking lot of a Dairy Queen dripping our cones, he saw a poster taped to the window:

FARMERS' COOPERATIVE
TRI-COUNTY ANNUAL
PICNIC
FOX VALLEY FAIRGROUNDS
AUGUST 15
Horseshoe pitching—Bingo
Sack races—Softball game
Egg throws—Distance swimming race
FOOD MUSIC REFRESHMENTS

He called us all over to see it and asked if we would like to go. For the next two weeks he swam whenever he could, and when he couldn't, he swam against his weights, newly slung from Wisconsin willows.

At the center of the Fox Valley Fairgrounds on the edge of Lake Winnebago, a game of baseball radiated motion slowly outward from the pitcher's mound. Farther out, under the trees, mothers rocked babies in covered buggies while fathers sipped beer and fussed with smoking stoves. The very old found shade at picnic tables and played games of cards. Smoke and music hung in the trees, then drifted through the high leaves to thin in the sunshine over the ball field and parking lots.

Our family was at a table by ten o'clock in the morning. Mother chose it for its location. From there she could watch the mainstand, the ball game, the road with its cars, the beach, and at the same time minister food and first-aid from a cooler and bags shaded under the table. From mid-morning to mid-afternoon we ran and played in the sun, ate and drank much, swam too much, until finally, exhausted, we had enough. That was at three o'clock. The swimming race was at four.

He had been at the beach since one. With us he had swum out to the raft, urging us along in the water with small praises until we reached up and found wood to hang on to. From a low diving board he did flips and jackknives. He arched into backdives, their incredible crescents thrilling us. Off and on for an hour we all lay with him on the raft, which rocked with our comings and goings, each departure bringing a plunge downward on that side of the raft and then a cool splash. Finally, the younger ones flopped into the water and swam back. Dangling his feet over the side, he sat with me and watched them work their way back to shore. Seeing that they were okay, he got to his feet and walked to the end of the diving board. He began to bounce in place, slowly at first, then higher and higher, until finally with each jump he was wiggling his legs madly, trying to keep his balance and land on the board. He kept it up, going still higher and then higher until, just when I was about to call to him, he bent his knees and slammed his feet to the board, shuddering it and riding it to a stop. He stood there thinking about something, not looking at me. He stared out over the lake for a long moment and then shallow-dived over the side and came up yards closer to shore. After a half-dozen strokes, he was walking on the beach.

At four o'clock the swimmers lined up on shore for the race. He was the first one in place. Bent at the waist, he wobbled his arms and long hair at the sand while the others, lined up beside him, laughed and talked with their friends. The president of the farmers' cooperative climbed up on the lifeguard stand to announce the race and explain the rules. The winner would be the one who swam the farthest. Out on the lake small boats bobbed, marking the course. Farther out, a cabin boat cruised back and forth. From somewhere a gunshot sounded and the small mob of men ran out and dove into the deeper water.

* * *

Watching the late-night stars and lights on the lake, we sat huddled with Mother on a bench that the sheriff had his men put on the beach for us. In the middle of us all, she sat ramrod-straight looking out at the lake. Men in swimming suits and deputies in uniforms moved around us, letting slip words like *weeds* and *cramp* and *drag,* despite their efforts to be quiet. At one point the sheriff moved among them talking and when he was through they were still. Then he stepped away from them to stand before Mother. "Ma'am," he said. "This could be a long night and I don't know what we might find, but from what I hear, your husband had that race won."

"My husband is an excellent swimmer," she said.

"Yes, ma'am," the sheriff said. "There is no doubt about that. I had a deputy here at this picnic today, and he said that from the gun your husband was so far out ahead of the others that they weren't even in the race. That he just swam. Said that he was out of sight. . ."

"My husband is an excellent swimmer," Mother said, and looked out to the lake.

"Yes, ma'am," the sheriff said, and then he and his badge and gun backed away behind the line of flashlights and lanterns.

Later, from far down the lake, barely visible at first, a single light bore steadily toward shore and then other lights from smaller boats drew toward and slowly formed a column behind it. They came slowly on for a long time until finally the smaller boats turned aside and the cabin boat bumped against a dock and stopped. There was a lifting then and a lowering, and a heavy blanket was carried and let down on the sand in front of Mother, and we children were led away.

Out in the middle of the pool, my son is practicing floating. He is clearly visible. There is no danger here. His belly rounded to the sky, he is all future. His grandfather, who he has never seen, is merely a lean man in the family album who had an accident. I've never told him more. It was a long time ago.

All around him, people are splashing and shouting. Some dive or jump from the board into the deep end. Others scream from the edges and then cannonball one another. Though he seems to be floating, I see that his hands are working furiously at his sides. Hoping that I've not left him with a fear of water, I get up from my bench and go to the edge of the pool. His eyes are wide now as he struggles to make his way from the middle to a wall. Thinking, *he had that race won,* I shout to him, "Don't be afraid. Roll over. Swim. Swim."